IT HAPPENED ONE FRIGHT

book eight of the matchmaker mysteries series

elise sax

It Happened One Fright (Matchmaker Mysteries – Book 8) is a work of fiction. Names, characters, places, and incidents are the products of the author's imagination or are used fictitiously. Any resemblance to actual events, locales, or persons, living or dead, is entirely coincidental.

ISBN: 978-1981216673
Published in the United States by Elise Sax

Cover design: Elizabeth Mackey
Edited by: Novel Needs
Formatted by: Jesse Kimmel-Freeman

Printed in the United States of America

elisesax.com
elisesax@gmail.com
http://elisesax.com/mailing-list.php
https://www.facebook.com/ei.sax.9
@theelisesax

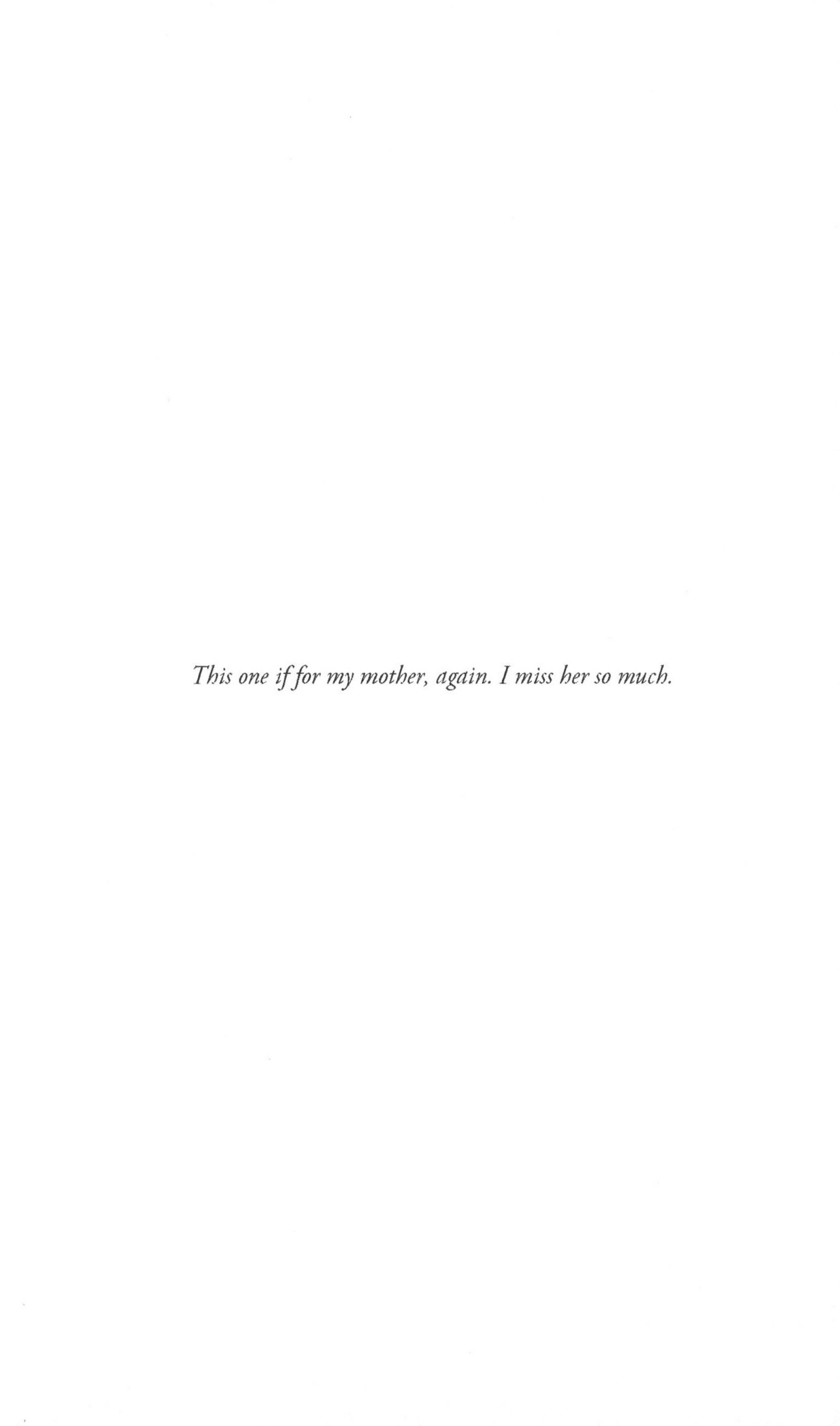

This one if for my mother, again. I miss her so much.

ALSO BY ELISE SAX

Five Wishes Series

Going Down
Man Candy
Hot Wired
Just Sacked
Wicked Ride
Five Wishes Series

Three More Wishes Series

Blown Away
Inn & Out
Quick Bang

Matchmaker Mysteries Series

An Affair to Dismember
Citizen Pain
The Wizards of Saws
Field of Screams
From Fear to Eternity
West Side Gory
Scareplane
It Happened One Fright
The Big Kill

Operation Billionaire

How to Marry a Billionaire
How to Marry Another Billionaire

Forever Series

Forever Now

Bounty
Switched
Moving Violations

CHAPTER 1 1
CHAPTER 2 13
CHAPTER 3 32
CHAPTER 4 47
CHAPTER 5 58
CHAPTER 6 81
CHAPTER 7 103
CHAPTER 8 118
CHAPTER 9 133
CHAPTER 10 157
CHAPTER 11 179
CHAPTER 12 193
CHAPTER 13 214
CHAPTER 14 234
CHAPTER 15 251
CHAPTER 16 264
ABOUT THE AUTHOR 286

CHAPTER 1

Life isn't fair, bubbeleh. At least that's what my mother always used to tell me. She also said that a dead rat under your bed meant that you were going to come into money. So, I learned to take or leave her advice. Yes, she had the gift, just like you and I. But just because you have a powerful third eye doesn't mean you can make heads or tails of it. You can't imagine the fakakta matches she made, dolly. Anyway, what was I talking about? Oh, yes. Life isn't fair. It's my belief that we think life isn't fair because it's full of the unexpected. Why is this happening to me? That's what we ask. This isn't what I had planned. That's what we say. We don't expect ninety-percent of what happens to us in life. There are surprises every day. So, tell your matches to turn their backs on life-isn't-fair and embrace the unexpected. Like a neighbor who drops by for a cup of coffee, let the unexpected in with a smile.

Lesson 121, Matchmaking advice from your Grandma Zelda

Spencer and I were a thing. We were practically living together. I had used his toothbrush on more than one occasion. So, I would have expected to become immune to his charms by now. At least, I should have stopped ogling him.

But here I was in the passenger seat of Spencer's car, studying his profile in the dark as he drove us off to our mystery location for our first vacation together. His nose was straight, and he had a strong jaw. I could just make out his long, black eyelashes as he blinked against the lights of the oncoming traffic. He was wearing a white, cotton button-down shirt and jeans.

I reached out and touched him. My fingers lightly traced the muscles on his upper arm, and then they traveled lower until they reached his lap.

"Pinky, I'm just a mortal man. If you keep it up, I'm going to crash this car."

I pulled my hand back.

"How much longer until we get there?" I asked. We had been driving for two hours, going up further into the mountains. We must have been about one hundred miles northeast of Cannes, California, where we lived.

"Not long, now. You don't want to spoil the surprise, do you?"

Since I had known Spencer, surprises usually came in the

form of murdered, dead people. I hated surprises. I wanted to live a life without them. Like Mr. Rogers' life with two pairs of shoes and a sweater for the afternoons. That kind of life. Nice and easy.

Serene.

Also, since Spencer had made such a big deal out of the surprise vacation, I had thought there was a sixty-to-seventy-five percent chance that we were going to Paris. In hindsight, I would have needed to get a passport for that, but the dream of eating French toast, French bread, and French fries on the Eiffel Tower, with Spencer maybe or maybe not wearing a beret, hadn't left me until we got in his car and drove east, in the opposite direction of the San Diego airport and flights to France.

The drive at night on the dark, mountain roads with Spencer hot and sexy next to me was already better than French bread, though. Riding off toward the romantic unknown was having a strong effect on me, like butterfly kisses on my erogenous zones.

"How much longer?" I repeated.

"Here we are," he said, pointing at a wooden sign on the side of the road, which was lit in light green.

"Love is a Splendored Thing Inn," I read. "For Lovers Who Crave Luxury."

"That's us, Pinky. Lovers who crave luxury."

I had never had luxury before, and I wasn't sure I was

craving it. But I was pretty sure I wouldn't snub my nose at it.

"What're we going to do here?" I asked and then a wave of red hot heat rushed through my body from my toes to my head. "I mean…" I started but let my voice trail off. It was pretty obvious what we were going to do at the inn, and I was glad I had gotten a bikini wax the day before. As we drove up the long, picturesque driveway, the inn came into view. It was large and white and very romantic. It was clear that this wasn't a sightseeing trip. This was a strawberries and champagne in a Jacuzzi bathtub trip.

Spencer put his hand between my thighs and gave my leg a gentle squeeze, which turned my insides into molten lava. "Oh," I breathed.

"This is going to be good," he promised. I believed him. Because Spencer was a terrible liar.

He parked in front of the inn and took our suitcases out of the trunk. I was only vaguely aware of the inn's décor, or even what the night manager said to us when we checked in. Instead, my brain was focused on the swirling cloud of hormones that had taken over my body. It focused on Spencer's hand on the small of my back. It focused on the way Spencer filled out his shirt and his jeans. And it focused on the way he stole glances at me, his eyes dark and full of desire.

Holy cow.

It was day one of our vacation. We had a full week away from home, away from work. It would be the first time in my adult life that I had a week where I could relax and not worry about money or what I wasn't doing. And I had a man who was in lov with me and who wanted to ravish me in the lobby.

That was obvious.

"I got us a suite," he told me as we left the elevator on t top floor of the inn. "with a Jacuzzi tub and a shower that you ne a Ph.D to work."

"It sounds like you've been here before. Like this is your to place for seducing women."

Spencer had been a ladies man before he finally set down with me. He had gone through more models than the F Modeling Agency. I had seen him with scads of skinny bitches perfect bone structure, and I didn't want to be a number at favorite love nest. The fear of being one of many cooled hormones, and suddenly I wanted to go home and watch *G Girls* reruns on TV while I ate chips in bed.

Spencer turned toward me and put his finger unde chin, tilting my head up. "Pinky, I've never been here before. did my research. I wanted to take you to the perfect place perfect time together."

He didn't blink. He fixed his eyes on communicating his truth to me. And again, I believed him.

Holy moly.

A door opened down the hall, and a young wom long t-shirt and panties hopped out, holding an ice bucket.

me. Just getting some ice." She giggled and skipped past us.

"Looks like we're not the only ones here for a perfect time," Spencer whispered in my ear. His breath was hot on my skin, but it made me shiver. He opened the door, and I walked in.

It was a beautiful room, with handwoven rugs on the wood floor, and a fire roaring in the fireplace. A king-sized bed was topped with rose petals, and champagne was chilling in an ice bucket next to two crystal glasses on a small table.

"It's perfect," I said, and Spencer scooped me up into his arms, as if I weighed nothing. "Are you taking me to the bed?" I asked. "I bet it's memory foam. I've always wanted to lie down on memory foam."

"I'm taking you to the shower."

"Why? Do I stink?"

It was a possibility. I was between perfumes. I just couldn't find one that I really liked at this point of my life, which included a secure job and committed relationship. As far as I knew, Chanel never created a scent for that.

"You smell wonderful, Pinky," Spencer told me, his voice deep and gravelly. "But prepare yourself because we're about to get very, very dirty."

He used my legs to open the bathroom door and flip on the lights.

"Dirty?" I breathed.

Spencer nodded. "Very, very dirty."

He put me down. My knees buckled, and he pulled me against him so I wouldn't fall. There was the familiar zing between us. Chemistry. If we could bottle it, we could make millions, selling it to despotic leaders who wanted to wage chemical war on the world.

My ears buzzed with arousal. Ditto my pores, which had sprouted goosebumps. If I tried to speak, I would have swallowed my tongue.

So, I didn't try to speak because I didn't want to swallow my tongue.

And I was going to need my tongue for other things.

"Are you okay?" Spencer asked me, slipping his hand under my shirt. He cupped my breast, and lightly caressed my nipple with his thumb.

"I might be having a stroke." My head flopped back, and my hands slapped Spencer's butt, clutching onto his firm butt cheeks like I was squeezing fresh orange juice.

He kissed my neck. "What are the symptoms?" he asked between kisses.

"There's throbbing."

"Mmm… Throbbing is good."

His hand traveled down my front until it was at just the right spot. "And quivering," I added.

"I like quivering."

In a swift bit of magic, Spencer transformed my lower half into complete nakedness, all the while maintaining contact with my special spot. "And heaving." I heaved. "Not throwing up heaving. The good kind of heaving."

"Like romance novel heaving," he said.

"What do you know about romance novels?" I asked. "You're way too macho to know anything about romance novels."

"Don't you know, Pinky, I *am* a romance novel."

And just like that, the rest of me was naked, and so was Spencer. Our clothes were pooled at our feet, a mound of fabric on the marble floor.

Spencer had been right about the shower. It was like something out of a science fiction movie with enough heads and nozzles and touch screen control panels to make a porn film starring Esther Williams. Not that she would do that. She was a nice lady who wouldn't have had anything to do with heads and nozzles that shot in every direction. She wasn't that kind of person. But I was totally that kind of person.

Totally.

Spencer adjusted the shower's controls to the honeymoon

setting, and we got in. Whoa, mama. It wasn't a shower. It was an experience. It was also a really good excuse to get down and dirty, just like Spencer had promised. His hands were everywhere, and so was his penis.

"Pinky, I'm so in love with you," he told me earnestly as he gazed into my eyes and rubbed up against my belly with his rigid manhood.

Spencer was really good at seduction.

All my fears of our vacation evaporated with Spencer's expert foreplay. Gone was the anxiety that Spencer would propose to me and that I wouldn't know how to react. Gone was my phobia of all things commitment, and tulle-covered wedding dresses. Banished was my concern that I hadn't packed correctly for a luxury vacation.

Now, my only thoughts were *oh* and *ah* and *yum*. I was in that space between consciousness and orgasm. Our hands raced to give each other pleasure, and Spencer positioned me to take me against the marble wall of the space age shower.

I was so ready.

I wanted him so much.

More than I wanted mint chocolate chip ice cream. And I wanted that real bad.

Spencer lifted me, and I wrapped my legs around him. "Nothing will stop me from making love to you, my beautiful

Pinky. We're made to be one. There's nothing in this world besides you and me."

"Oh, yes," I breathed and pressed my lips against his.

That's when we heard the noise. It came from the other room. Spencer turned his head, breaking our kiss. "Did you hear that?"

"No," I lied. "Don't stop touching me. I'm so close."

He kissed me again, but stopped a moment later when there was another noise.

A scream.

Spencer put me down and shook his index finger in my face. "You stay here," he growled, his authoritarian voice on full strength.

"You're not going out there, are you?"

"I'm a cop, Pinky."

And that said it all. He walked out of the shower, his body tensed, like he was prepared for any emergency. There had been one scream and one boom and that was it. But it had definitely come from our hotel room. Spencer put his hand on the door knob and turned. I squeezed the water out of my curly hair and walked out of the shower.

"No, Gladys," Spencer growled. "Stay here."

"Okay," I lied. "And don't call me Gladys."

The romance had left the room. The cloud of hormones had dissipated, and now I was just wet. And not in a good way.

"I mean it, Pinky. You stay here."

"I said, okay."

He opened the door and stepped into the room. I followed him.

Ever since my father died when I was a little girl, I had been squeamish. I couldn't even think of blood without passing out or at least getting woozy. But ever since I had moved to Cannes to help my grandmother with her matchmaking business, I had had more than my share of encounters with dead, murdered people. I had even touched a couple of them.

The experiences had definitely hardened me, and I had acquired a tolerance for a certain amount of gore and the harshness of life. But nothing prepared me for the sight I saw in our luxury, king-sized bed with a hand-crafted quilt and memory foam mattress.

In fact, I didn't register much before I lost consciousness. The only thing I knew was that there was a murdered woman lying on my side of the bed, and she was dead. Obviously dead. And obviously murdered in a horrible way. It was the young woman who had skipped down the hall in search of ice, and now she had been brutally murdered in the perfect bed of my perfect vacation with my perfect man.

"Dead. Bed. Woman. Ice. Dead." I moaned.

With that, I passed out. Cold.

CHAPTER 2

Warts aren't so bad. Even on a nose...not so bad, bubbeleh. I've been in the business for a lot of years, and I've heard a lot of complaining. "He wore pleated pants." "She parted her hair in the middle." "He had a space between his two front teeth." Give me a break. What do any of these things have to do with love? Bupkis, dolly. Bupkis. The same thing with warts and pimples and all the little things that matches focus on except for what counts. As a matchmaker, you have to explain to them what counts, dolly. And that's love. Love's what counts.

Lesson 74, Matchmaking advice from your
Grandma Zelda

I didn't dream. I didn't struggle to wake up. Instead, I regained consciousness like I was waking from a relaxing nap.

"There you are," Spencer said, an obvious look of relief on his face. He was naked from his waist up, with his lower half wrapped in a towel. Still wet, his hair dripped water onto my cheek. I wiped it off.

"Looks like she's been stabbed a good forty times," I heard a man say in the room.

"Who's here?" I touched my body, panicked that I was lying naked on the floor while other men were in the room, but Spencer had covered me with a couple of towels.

"Emergency services. Are you sure you're all right?"

"Yes, of course," I said, even though I had fainted.

"Let me help you up."

I clutched onto Spencer's arms. "Don't let me see. Don't let me see."

He understood what I was talking about. "I'm going to walk you back into the bathroom. You won't see a thing."

Carefully, he wrapped me in the towels as I got up so that nobody would see me naked. I averted my gaze from the bed, but I could tell that the room was filled with law enforcement, and a group of people surrounded the bed, studying the scene of the crime.

I walked into the bathroom, and Spencer closed the door behind me, while he stayed on the other side of the room. I assumed that he had to talk to law enforcement and explain to them why a murdered woman was in our bed.

Good luck with that.

I couldn't figure it out. Did the ice woman wander into our room, and the killer murdered her, thinking she was me? I shuddered. I didn't like that reason. Or maybe the killer chased her into our room and killed her there? That was a more appetizing option, as far as I was concerned. Or maybe she was murdered somewhere else and dropped in our bed to frame us. That wasn't an attractive prospect, considering my aversion to being in prison. Whatever the reason, it didn't look good for us. I could see the headlines: Murder in the Love Nest. I could almost feel the handcuffs on me, already.

I got dressed and looked in the mirror. My mascara had run down my face from the erotic shower. I cleaned off my face and ran a hotel comb through my hair as far as I could. My hair was a lot tougher than the comb, and three of the comb's teeth broke off somewhere in my wet locks.

"Maybe I'm dreaming," I told my reflection. "Maybe I fell asleep and dreamed that a woman was murdered in my bed." I gave my arm a hard pinch. Ouch. Damn it. I was wide awake.

"Dolly."

I jumped three feet in the air and crashed back to the floor, clutching onto the marble counter for balance. In the mirror, my grandmother was standing, looking at me.

And Grandma didn't look good. She was pale and clutching her chest.

"Dolly, I need you," she said, her voice a hoarse whisper. "Hurry. Come now."

I turned around, but my grandmother wasn't in the bathroom. I turned back around to the mirror, and she wasn't there, either. But she had been there. At least she had been there in my mind.

Holy cow. I had had a vision.

I touched the spot between my eyes, half-expecting to find a third eye. But nope. Nothing there except for the beginnings of some heavy-duty, what-the-hell lines. Was this the way it started? Knowing things that couldn't be known?

What did I know?

I knew that my grandmother needed me. I knew it as surely as I knew that okra was slimy no matter how it was cooked and that Adam Sandler movies were totally overrated.

I slammed the bathroom door open. "Spencer, we have to leave. Now! We have to go home. Grandma needs me!"

Local law enforcement didn't want to let us leave, but as Police Chief of a close by, bigger town, Spencer convinced them to accept a rushed statement and a promise to answer any further questions if needed.

And away we went.

"Speed!" I urged Spencer as he whisked us away from the scene of the crime to possibly another scene of the crime.

"What's happening? What's happening?" Spencer asked, as he took the thirty-mile-an-hour turns at sixty miles an hour. Trees whizzed by as we traveled to Cannes in record time.

"My grandmother needs me!" I shouted.

"I don't understand. Are you becoming like her?"

Becoming like her. We both knew what that meant, but we had never exactly talked about what Grandma was like. She just was.

"I don't think so," I said, but I didn't sound convincing. Actually, I had no idea. It could have been a one-shot deal. It could have been some kind of psychic push from my grandmother, like E.T. calling home. Or I could have been seeing things, which was the most likely truth.

But something in me told me not to listen to the most likely truth. Something in me told me to make Spencer go even faster.

"Can't we just call her?" Spencer asked.

"No," I said, but I didn't know why.

"This is the first time you haven't gone ape-shit over a murder. Normally, you're in high Miss Marple mode at this point. You didn't ask one question about the murdered girl."

He was right. My concern over my grandmother had superseded my Miss Marple curiosity and compulsion to solve mysteries. Or maybe my Miss Marple was broken.

"There!" I shouted when I saw the sign for Cannes, California. Population 2501. Elevation 4226 feet.

"I know, Pinky. I've been here before."

"Turn left here!"

"I know, Pinky."

Spencer drove up the driveway, and I jumped out of the car before he turned off the motor. I opened the door and ran inside the house.

The place was packed with people, as usual. My grandmother's house was the center of the action in town. Because she was a matchmaker and a shut-in, those searching for love and community organizing were forced to go to her. And they were never disappointed.

However, it was late at night to have so much action at her house. Normally things wound down by seven in the evening. Now it was closer to nine, and every folding chair was out in the parlor, and the mayor was lecturing the horde of volunteers.

"This is going to take every ounce of our egg boiling and egg dyeing abilities. It's like D-Day, but harder and much more important. Much more important!"

"Eggs are more important than D-Day," Meryl, the blue-haired librarian sneered. The mayor wasn't known for his intellectual strengths. I had heard something about an epic Easter egg hunt this year, and I figured the meeting had something to do with that.

"Meryl, where's Grandma?" I asked, interrupting the meeting. All heads turned to me, surprise plastered on their faces. The whole town knew that Spencer and I were supposed to be away on a super romantic vacation, and my early return would definitely be the number one gossip topic for a while.

"She's in the sunroom with a client," Meryl told me. Spencer walked into the house, and he followed me when I ran through the kitchen to the sunroom.

Grandma was there with a huge man, sitting next to him on the yellow cushions of the sunroom couch. "Nobody understands me," he said with a thick Japanese accent. "Women don't want me."

Grandma took his hand. "You are a beautiful, talented sumo wrestler. I know that there's a woman in Cannes who will recognize your specialness. You will be understood. And you will be loved."

Spencer came up behind me. He put his hands on my shoulders, his chin on the top of my head, and sighed a sigh of relief. I realized that I had been holding my breath, and I sighed, too. Grandma looked fine. She was doing a matchmaking consultation, the first step in finding love for a client.

The sumo wrestler stood. He was a nice-looking man, and there was lots of him. He towered over my grandmother and seemed to take up the entire sunroom. He was wearing a massive blue suit with a tie tied into a Windsor knot.

Everything was fine.

Then, Grandma turned, and we locked eyes. She nodded ever so slightly, and at that moment, I knew I had been right. She needed me. Something horrible was about to happen. A small tear rolled down her face, and I ran to her.

I learned something that day. There was a difference between a heart attack and a heart event. An event was better than an attack, or so the doctor said. Still, he wanted my grandmother to go to the hospital, but since she never left her property, she refused to go.

Luckily there was a sumo wrestler around when Grandma clutched her chest and keeled over. He caught her easily and swept her up into his enormous arms. I ran to her, and miraculously, I kept a clear head. While, running, I whipped my cellphone out of my purse and dialed the doctor. Then, I was a drill sergeant, ordering the wrestler to carry her to her room and Spencer to get her cold water. And then we waited and prayed and made deals with God to take care of my grandmother.

God came through. Either that or it wasn't her time. Either that or my grandmother was strong as a horse.

In any case, by midnight my grandmother was tucked into her bed, comfortable and high on tranquilizers. The house was cleared of guests with promises to make at least two thousand casseroles. And Spencer turned around in circles, unused to not being useful. Finally, I urged him to go to bed, and I wrapped myself in a quilt and curled up in the chair next to my grandmother's bed.

"You're a good girl," Grandma told me, slightly slurring her speech.

"Are you comfortable? Do you need something?"

"I'm fine, bubbeleh."

"But…" I wanted to ask her if she was going to stay fine, or if I should start crying and never stop, if she would continue to be there for me, or if I would be an orphan. But I couldn't bring myself to say the words. I was such a coward.

"Dolly, I've always been hazy about myself, you know," she said. My throat grew thick, and I willed my eyes not to fill up with tears, but they didn't obey me. "But I have the feeling that I'm going to be up and ready to match folks in about ten days."

I wiped my eyes with the quilt. "Really? How strong of a

feeling do you have? Like a for sure feeling? Or just a so-so kinda feeling?"

"Ten days," she said and started to snore.

I sat up in my chair. "Wait a second. Ten days? You're going to be in bed for ten days? So, who's going to be in charge of the matchmaking? I can't do it for ten days. Grandma? Grandma?"

She was out and snoring like she was trying to inhale the sheets. I should have been exhausted, but I was wide awake with the panic that only filling Grandma's shoes for ten days could provoke.

"Honey, you need a peel. I've never let my face look like what you've got going on. Come into the salon pronto."

"Huh?" I asked, waking up. I had fallen asleep in a pretzel position, and I had a crick in my neck. There was a pool of drool on my arm. I cracked my eyes open to find Grandma's room filled with Bird, who owned the local salon, and two of her estheticians. They got to work, washing Grandma's hair and getting her ready for the day. She was going to look better, recuperating from a heart event in bed than I was going to look in perfect health.

"You got some grays, you know, Gladie," Bird told me, pointing at my head.

My hand flew to the top of my head. "I do not. Take that

back, Bird."

"You need to come into the salon. You need a full day. It's an emergency. You've let yourself go. I would have thought you'd have spruced yourself up for the big third finger, left hand trip with the hot cop."

I rubbed my neck. "I wasn't on a third finger, left hand trip. Where did you hear that? That's a total lie," I lied.

"You come into the salon, and I'll get you buffed up. It might take a power sander, but we'll get your skin back on track. What are you eating these days, Gladie?"

"Not much." I had eaten a family pack of Double Stuff Oreos for breakfast the day before, but that was stress eating, which didn't count.

"I'm on the 1950s diet. Awesome diet. Lots of green Jello."

"That doesn't sound too bad," I said, sitting up, straighter.

"Dolly, I haven't had coffee, yet," Grandma said from her bed. "Would you get your grandma breakfast?"

"Sure, Grandma," I said, getting up.

"Add a leftover thigh from Chik'n Lik'n. There's a bucket in the refrigerator. And a bagel with cream cheese, of course. There might be a cherry Danish somewhere, too."

"Okay, Grandma."

I guessed heart events made a person hungry.

"The Easter Egg committee will be here in an hour, bubbeleh," Grandma told me.

Oh, geez. For a brief, wonderful moment, I had forgotten that I was now in charge of Zelda's matchmaking business. That meant that I was pretty much in charge of the whole town.

Had the world gone crazy?

I couldn't be in charge of a town. I couldn't even be in charge of my debit card.

I hurried to my bathroom to pee. Spencer was lying in bed in sweatpants and no shirt, while he watched *Simpsons* reruns and laughed, pointing at the television screen. "How's Zelda?" he asked me through the bathroom door.

"Hungry. I have to feed her and then I have the Easter Egg committee to deal with."

I put a brush through my hair and tied it into a ponytail. I went back in my bedroom and stripped out of my dirty underwear.

"Sounds rough," Spencer said, absentmindedly watching me as I got dressed again in jeans and a t-shirt.

I turned on him, my eyes twitching. "Rough? It's a catastrophe. I'm going to ruin everything. I can't do this."

Spencer muted the TV and got out of bed. "I don't want to alarm you, Pinky, but you might be having a seizure."

"Don't you think I know that? It's everything I can do not to swallow my tongue right now. Any minute, you're going to have to shove a spoon in my mouth. And I don't want to even start on the blood thingies in my brain that are hemorrhaging."

Spencer arched an eyebrow and smirked his little smirk and pulled me into an embrace. "That's rough about the blood thingies in your brain," he said. "I know a cure for blood thingies." He rubbed up against me to highlight his cure.

I pushed him away. "You're five years old, Spencer. This is serious. I have responsibilities now. For ten days."

"That sucks, Pinky. Does that mean that little Spencer is going to be lonely for ten days?"

He hopped back onto the bed and clicked the unmute button. *The Simpsons* roared to life. "Is that what you're doing all day?"

"Hey, I'm on vacation, Pinky. You want to join me?"

I stood over him, open-mouthed, watching him stare at the television, completely relaxed. He was totally happy. He wasn't filled with panic, anxiety, and low self-esteem. He didn't have to deal with the Easter egg committee. He didn't have to match a sumo wrestler. I wanted to hit him with a hammer. If only I had a hammer. Why didn't I have a hammer?

I stomped my foot and wagged my finger at him. "You're being insensitive. You're being unhelpful. You're being a man!"

"I'm trying to be a man, Pinky. Little Spencer is trying to be a man, too. Poor Little Spencer. You hurt his feelings."

"Oh. I'm sorry."

"You are? Come on and make it up to Little Spencer."

I threw my dirty underpants at him. It didn't have the same effect as a hammer, but he got the point.

After I fed my grandmother, I had forty minutes before the invasion was due to happen. I had plenty of time to get coffee, especially if I took my car. It was a no-brainer. I needed a real latte before it was time to crash and burn and face my failure.

I got a half block away from Tea Time, the tea shop where I bought my coffee, before police car lights flashed in my rearview mirror and sirens went off. "What the hell?" I said and pulled to the side of the road.

I turned off my motor and watched as Terri Williams stepped out of the police car and sauntered toward me. Oh, crap. Terri had recently moved to Cannes as its newest detective on the police force. But she had screwed up and was demoted to a beat cop.

And she hated me.

She hated me so much.

I wasn't crazy about her, either. She was a heinous bitch. But it made me crazy that she hated me. How could she hate me? I was the nicest person in the world. Nobody hated me. Even people who had tried to kill me didn't hate me. I was a very likable person. At least I hoped I was.

Terri tapped on my window, and I rolled it down.

"Hi, Terri. How are you? You look great today." I wasn't lying. Terri was one of the most beautiful women I had ever seen. Oh, who was I kidding? She was definitely the number one most beautiful woman I had ever seen. Even in her disgusting uniform, she was stunningly gorgeous.

"License, registration, and proof of insurance," she said.

"Do I have a taillight out?"

"License, registration, and proof of insurance," she repeated, louder.

I rifled through my purse and gave her my license. "I think the registration is in the glove compartment. I'm not really good with paperwork. You know how it is, right?" I laughed and tapped her arm.

"Don't touch a police officer," she warned. "Are you saying that you don't have registration for this vehicle?"

"Of course I do." She scribbled on her ticket pad. "What are you doing there? Are you giving me a ticket?"

"Listen, Ms. Burger, it's none of your business what I'm doing. I'm in charge, not you. Do you have the proper paperwork for this vehicle?"

She continued to write on her ticket pad. I opened the glove compartment and searched through it. "I don't know who put the candy bar wrappers in here," I told her. "Pretty funny, though. Do you like chocolate? I love chocolate. Funny thing about chocolate that not a lot of people know..."

"If you delay this any longer, I'm going to take you in and put you on a seventy-two-hour hold."

She was such a bitch.

"Eureka!" I shouted, finding the registration. I handed it to her, and she inspected it like it was garbage. "Nice weather we're having," I said, brightly, showing her all of my teeth. "April in Cannes. Am I right?"

It was hard to be nice to a woman who wasn't nice. I couldn't figure out how to win her over and make her like me.

"So why did you pull me over, not that I'm complaining?" I asked. "Not complaining a bit. I have total respect for law enforcement. Love the law. The law is the best. Nothing better than the law. Law is the tops. Woohoo law!" I shouted, shaking my fist at the car's ceiling.

Terri handed me back my license and registration and gave me a ticket. "Three-hundred-dollars?" I shrieked. "Why? For what?"

"It's written right there. Have a nice day."

"I can't read this. It's like a doctor's handwriting. Young driving? You ticketed me for young driving?"

Terri studied her fingernails. "Annoying driving. You were ticketed for annoying driving."

"That's a thing? That's real?"

"It is now."

My first instinct was to claw her eyes out. But I had short fingernails, and she had a gun. There was also the problem that if I wanted her to like me, it probably wouldn't help my case if I attacked her through the open driver's side window.

The thing was that this wasn't the first ticket Terri had given me since she had been demoted. I had four other tickets crammed on the bottom of my purse. Spencer could probably take care of them, but I had a secret fear that when faced with the choice of me and Hot Mama Terri, he would choose her. After all, she had gone to college, and the other four tickets were for speeding, changing lanes without signaling, and two for rolling through a stop sign while I was applying mascara. Spencer would have given me hell if he saw those tickets.

The key to solving my problems was to win Terri over. Somehow, I had to make her like me.

"What the hell is that?" Terri asked staring down the street.

It was the shoe salesman Jonas Finklemeyer driving a

motorized couch down the street. At this point, as a resident of Cannes, not much could surprise me. Sure, I had never seen a motorized couch before, but I had seen stranger.

"I don't know," I lied.

Terri seemed to brace herself for impact. She stared at the two-seater motorized couch with orange and black upholstery. Finally, I had a way to ingratiate myself with her. I opened my door and stepped out.

"Let me help you," I said.

"I don't want your help."

"Yes, you do. You just don't know you do. Believe me, I can help with this."

"I don't want your help."

"Yes, you do."

"If you help me, I'll shoot you."

I laughed. "Oh, Terri. You slay me."

I walked into the middle of the street and waved my hands at Jonas Finklemeyer. "Jonas! Stop!"

"Hello, Gladie!" he called back. "How's Zelda?"

"Oh, you know," I yelled over the hum of his couch's motor. "Fine. You think you could stop?"

"Probably not. The brakes aren't working."

The couch continued to roll down the street, picking up speed as it reached an incline.

"What did he say?" Terri asked me.

"He said he can't stop."

"The hell he can't. I'll shoot his ass if he doesn't."

Terri took her gun out of the holster and aimed it at Jonas.

CHAPTER 3

We are a hungry people and getting hungrier every day. There's a lot of supersizing going on, bubbeleh. This is called biting off more than you can chew. It's dangerous business, dolly, and we all do it. More, more, more. Sometimes more isn't more. I mean, it's more, but it's too much. And then we choke. So, when you're matchmaking, take it one step at a time. One step at a time. Don't choke.

Lesson 102, Matchmaking advice from your Grandma Zelda

My heart pounded in my chest. I didn't want to see Jonas mowed down with bullets on Main Street. He was a nice guy. He regularly gave me thirty-percent off floor model shoes in his shop.

Of course, if he died, there would be a hell of a clearance sale, and there was a pair of suede boots I wanted to have.

Hell. I was so going to hell. I was weighing a man's death with my need for discounted suede boots. I was no better than Terri. But I didn't want to go to hell. I wanted to be a nice person. I needed to save Jonas.

"This is for your own good," I told Terri and rammed her like I was a linebacker for the Pittsburgh Steelers. She was fit, but she couldn't have been more than one hundred and ten pounds. I knocked her off her feet, and the gun flew out of her hand, up into the air, and landed on the sidewalk across the street.

I had successfully saved Jonas Finklemeyer. I had done a good deed. I wasn't going to hell.

"Oh my God!" Terri shouted and shielded her face. At first I didn't know what she was shielding herself from, but then I realized that the couch was coming fast, and she was about to be run over.

"You better move!" Jonas yelled. "This couch has a mind of its own!"

"I'll save you, Terri! Gladie to the rescue!"

Like David Banner turning into The Incredible Hulk, I grabbed Terri's hands and yanked her up, tossing her like a shot putter in the Olympics.

But good intentions aren't always the best, and my aim was off. Since I wasn't really David Banner, I only managed to move her a few feet, which turned out to be the exact distance to Jonas's motorized couch.

I watched in shock and horror as Terri flew onto the couch. "What the hell is happening?" Terri shouted.

"We're going to crash!" Jonas answered, screaming.

He wasn't wrong. A few seconds later, the couch rammed into a light pole. Somehow, Jonas managed to hold onto the couch, but little Terri Williams flew like an eagle past the pole, flapping her arms wildly until she made contact with a stop sign and fell to the ground.

"Well," I muttered. "That didn't work out exactly as I had planned."

I crossed my fingers and prayed that she was okay and wouldn't shoot me. Miraculously, she stood up and focused her anger at Jonas.

"You better have a permit to drive that thing, or you're going to be in so much trouble!" she shouted at him while she flipped her ticket book open.

"You probably don't want me here," I said, tiptoeing back to my car. I got in and started it up fast. "It was nice seeing you again, Terri," I said in a whisper and drove off.

It had been my first effort to make Terri like me, and it didn't exactly go perfectly, but at least I wasn't in jail, and she could still walk.

I parked in front of Tea Time. Next door to the tea shop, there was some kind of construction going on, and there were construction guys coming and going. I had about five minutes to get home before the Easter egg hunt committee arrived. I couldn't let my grandmother down.

I opened the door to Tea Time. It was packed to the rafters. The tea shop was housed in an old saloon with real bullet holes in the wall and the original bar still intact and shiny. The shop was owned by an ornery octogenarian named Ruth, who despised coffee drinkers, but she made the best lattes in the world. I had struck a deal with her for free lattes for a year.

"Latte, Ruth!" I called, pushing my way through the crowd to the bar. "Make it a large, pronto."

I slapped my hand on the bar counter. Ruth rounded on me with a teapot in her hand. "Don't you see that I'm busy with real customers?" she asked. "This world of twittering and bookfacing has turned every half-decent person into a card-carrying Ayn Rand pain in the ass. You think you're better than a hard-working member of the AFL-CIO. Cutting in line like you own the place. Fascist coffee drinker. What kind of coffee do you want? Hazelnut Atlas Shrugged freshly ground from Nazi Germany? Huh? Huh?"

"Ruth, the only words I understood were 'pain in the ass' and 'cutting in line.'"

"Excuse me, ma'am, my tea, please?" a man asked, nicely, leaning against the bar.

"I'm getting to you," she screeched at him. "You see that I have your teapot in my hand, ready to give it to you."

"I see that, but I thought you forgot about me because you're talking with this woman," he said.

She threw up her hands. "That's it. That's it. Even tea drinkers have gone to the dark side. Now you're going to have to wait for your tea while I make her a latte. You have no one to blame but yourself."

"But you've got the teapot in your hand," he pointed out, wisely. Fool. It didn't pay to be wise with Ruth. It was better to just suffer her abuse and get served, preferably with homemade chocolate chip scones.

"You better sit down if you ever want to taste tea again," she told him between her clenched teeth. "Now, tell me what the hurry is, Gladie. Does this have something to do with your grandma?"

At the mention of my grandmother, emotion choked me, and I could only nod, yes. Ruth laid her hand on mine. "That woman has been gorging herself on junk food since she learned to open her mouth. If that hasn't killed her, a little heart business sure isn't."

"The doctor said it was just a heart event," I said. "Not a heart attack. So, you think she'll be okay?"

I didn't know why I was asking Ruth, but I guessed I was looking for assurance wherever I could find it.

"That woman hasn't butted into the life of her last victim, yet. She's much too much of a buttinski to give up the ghost,"

Ruth said.

She had a point. My grandmother was a major buttinski. She would have done anything to keep sticking her nose into everyone's lives. "She's not a buttinski, Ruth. You take that back. And get me my latte. I've got an Easter egg hunt committee coming any minute."

"Holy crap, Gladie. You better wear a bullet-proof vest for that. Have you heard what they want to do with that crazy hunt?"

"No, what?"

She didn't answer me. She looked past me, and her face dropped. I turned around. A man in a red hard hat had entered and was marching right toward her.

"What now?" she demanded.

"We broke the water main. We should be able to get it back online by the end of the day."

"Oh, you will, will you," she said, her voice chock full of menace. She brandished a tea towel like a weapon and walked around the bar, in order to get into the construction worker's face, which was about a foot above hers.

She barked at him about coffee, and I realized I wasn't going to get my coffee in time. I would have to handle the Easter egg hunt committee.

I went home, coffee-less.

I was late. The committee had already arrived, and without the steadying force of my grandmother, the house was filled with chaos and mayhem. I heard them before I opened the door. Despite my strong desire to run away, I took a deep, healing breath and opened it.

"World record!" Mayor Robinson shouted.

"Has your last screw gotten loose?" a woman asked him, shaking her fist at him. She would have probably punched him, but Spencer was standing in between them, ostensibly to protect the mayor. "You want us to hide five-hundred-thousand eggs?"

"Five-hundred and one thousand, in order to clinch the record," the mayor told her.

"I don't have that many pots to boil eggs," she screeched.

"This will put us on the map. The map! And they want to put me on TV. I'm getting a facial peel and my teeth whitened for my appearance."

"How about we all sit down?" Spencer asked. "It's better to discuss eggs while sitting down. I can't believe I just said that," he added, running his fingers through his thick hair.

The door opened behind me, and the committee members noticed me for the first time. I waved to them like an idiot. "Gladie what do you think about this idea to put Cannes on the map?" the mayor asked me.

"Uh," I said.

The familiar scent of expensive perfume wafted up my nose, and one of my best friends, Lucy Smythe, walked up behind me and put her arm around my shoulder. "What did I miss? Please tell me I didn't miss anything. I heard that the town was going to hard-boil every egg this side of the Mississippi."

Ahead, Spencer mouthed "help" to me. I was on. I stepped into the parlor and pretended I was Grandma.

What would my grandmother do? It was a philosophical question, but one I should have been able to answer since I had been watching her for a good chunk of my life. There was no way I could be my grandmother. Despite her saying I had the gift, there was no evidence of that. But I could pretend that I was her. I was good at pretending.

I plastered a serene Zelda smile on my face and sat down on one of the folding chairs. "How many eggs do we normally use in an Easter egg hunt?" I asked the mayor. Spencer's face was the picture of relief, and he ducked out of the parlor at the speed of light. I wanted to go with him, but somehow I was cursed with a burst of maturity, which kept my butt in the chair. Lucy sat down next to me, and unlike mine, her smile was real. Nothing made her happier than Cannes craziness.

"Two hundred," one of the committee members answered. Her name was Josephine, if I had remembered correctly. "Two hundred eggs. It's not like we're bursting at the seams with children here, you know."

She was right. Cannes wasn't children-centric. We got influxes of kids with the tourists, but we didn't have roving bands of Mommy & Me classes or anything.

"I've got that worked out," the mayor said, smiling. "We'll invite children to come to the world's biggest Easter egg hunt. We'll have a celebrity guest, games, and prizes."

It didn't sound half bad. Normally, the mayor was dumber than spit, but somehow he managed to work out a good idea, as far as I could make out. "That sounds like a lot of fun," I commented.

"Is that Zelda's official position on this whole thing?" Josephine asked. "Are you speaking for her?"

I was supposed to be speaking for her, but I had no idea what her official position was. I didn't want to make waves. If I had been smart, I would have walked upstairs and asked her. But I didn't want to pester her about hard-boiled eggs, and I had promised to give her a break for ten days. Was that so much to ask? Well, yes, of course it was a lot to ask, but I didn't want to let her down, and I didn't want to look like a wimp in front of the Easter egg hunt committee.

"Yes," I heard myself say. "I speak for my grandmother, and I think it's a lovely idea. The world record for largest Easter egg hunt. Lots of children and prizes and a celebrity. Why not?"

Josephine threw her hands up. "Okay, then. Hear that group? We have logistics to deal with."

It was a moment of victory for me. I had managed my first challenge like a pro. I hopped up and a down a little in my seat and almost clapped my hands in glee. Lucy leaned over and whispered in my ear.

"Easter Sunday is in eight days, Gladie."

My head whipped around to her. "Are you joking?" What did I know about Easter? I barely knew about Passover.

Lucy shrugged. "Eight days, darlin'. Five-hundred-and-one-thousand eggs, boiled, dyed, and hidden. Someone should warn the chickens to get to work."

I swallowed, but I found it difficult because my throat had gotten thick. The mayor was deep in conversation with Josephine, suggesting that they boil the eggs outside to save time. All of a sudden, it dawned on me that I had just agreed with what had to be the dumbest man in Cannes.

"I haven't had coffee, yet," I explained to Lucy.

"You probably shouldn't do that, again, darlin'. I mean, go to a committee meeting before you caffeine up."

It turned out that breaking the world's record for biggest Easter egg hunt was a crazy undertaking, and it would have to be all hands on deck to get it done. The rest of the meeting dealt with logistics, planning, and schedules. I was no help, and after about twenty minutes, I made an excuse about Grandma and matchmaking and snuck upstairs with Lucy.

Bird and her team were finishing up my grandmother's beauty treatment, and Meryl the librarian had shown up to make sure Grandma would take a morning nap and then eat lunch with her in the bedroom. Spencer had brought his television into her room and hooked it up. It had to have been a huge sacrifice for him. No *Family Guy* or *Simpsons* during his vacation, stuck at his girlfriend's grandmother's house without a thing to watch while she convalesced from a heart event.

"Thank you," I mouthed to him, as he turned the television to home shopping, which was Meryl's favorite station. Spencer handed her the remote control.

"The committee meeting is going over logistics," I reported to my grandmother. "How are you feeling?"

"Ready for a nap," she said. Her face was pale and ashen.

"Is the doctor coming today?" I asked.

"Two o'clock. Meryl, remind him to bring eggs. Gladie, let Josephine know that Walley's has a special on eggs this week."

Her eyes closed. "Okay, Grandma," I whispered. I hugged myself, trying to bear the worried feeling I had for her. Spencer put his arm around my waist and pulled me into his side.

With my grandmother drifting off, everyone left the room, except for Meryl, who sat next to the bed and watched a woman sell hangers on television. Spencer closed the bedroom door, gently. Bird waved goodbye and went back to her salon with her team.

"I guess we could go to lunch," Spencer suggested.

Lucy took my hand. "I get her first. We're lunching with Bridget."

"We are?" I asked.

"Yep."

Spencer's face dropped. "You don't want a handsome man tagging along?"

"Oh, darlin'. That sounds like a real treat, but wouldn't you prefer to watch the fight on the big screen with Uncle Harry?" Lucy asked.

Spencer's face brightened immediately. Uncle Harry was Lucy's new husband, and despite the name, wasn't related to her except by marriage. "Does he have hoagies?"

"No," Lucy said. "He's got a guy coming over to grill some thick ribeyes. How does that sound?"

"I'll get my shoes," he said, kissed me, and ran back to our room.

"Men are so easy to please," Lucy said. I had recently discovered that Lucy used to be a high-priced call girl, so I assumed she knew exactly what it took to please men. Now she was retired and only had to please one man, but she still had charm up the wazoo for everyone else.

"I think I have matchmaking to do," I told her.

"Gladie, everyone's got to eat. Besides, we have to catch up."

"You saw me yesterday."

"Exactly. I helped you pack for your romantic vacation, and now, here you are. So, you have to update me."

"Oh."

"And we have to get Bridget out of her house and into Saladz for a good lunch. I'm worried about her."

Our friend Bridget Donovan was seven months pregnant and a bookkeeper in the last week of tax season. She had been working nonstop.

"Can we stop for coffee first?" I asked Lucy.

"Of course! But we should take the long way around the Historic District. You won't believe what I saw on Main Street."

I would have bet it had something to do with a motorized couch, but I decided to keep Lucy in the dark about my participation in that particular disaster.

We drove off in Lucy's Mercedes, and it wasn't until we were parked and standing at Tea Time's door that I remembered about the water main. Ruth had stuck a sign to the front door. *Closed because of corporate devils, who are taking over the world with their craptastic coffee.*

"When do you think Ruth will start to soften?" Lucy

asked, reading the sign.

"Maybe five years after she's dead."

"What does she mean about the corporate devils?"

"I think that would be me," a man wearing a hard hat said, walking toward us from the construction zone next door. He smiled wide. "I do take umbrage over the criticism of my coffee, however. I make the world's best lattes, and that's a fact. May I make you one? On me?"

"What do you mean?" I asked, suspicious. It wasn't every day that a strange man offered to make me coffee. In fact, this was the first time.

"I'm Ford Essex, owner of Buckstars, the new, best coffee place in Cannes."

"You're opening a coffee place next to Tea Time?" I asked. It was the craziest thing I had ever heard. It was like opening a Jewish deli next to the KKK headquarters. It was a declaration of war. It was suicide.

There was no way I was going anywhere near Ford Essex. Ruth was going to explode all over him, and the shrapnel was going to take down innocents in a ten-mile radius. I couldn't afford to be murdered now when the world's biggest Easter egg hunt was only eight days away.

But it looked like Lucy's curiosity was stronger than her survival instinct. She put her hand out like Scarlett O'Hara. "I've always depended on the kindness of strangers," she gushed. "We would love to."

CHAPTER 4

Look sharp. That's what a matchmaker must do. Not just your two eyes, dolly. Look sharp deep into your matches. Feel their feelings. Fear their fears. Hope their hopes. It's more than walking around in their shoes, bubbeleh. It's knowing their essence. Look sharp. And listen. And feel. There's a story they need to tell, but they don't know how.

Lesson 44, Matchmaking advice from your
Grandma Zelda

As we walked into the store next to Tea Time, the workers were hammering in the Buckstars sign overhead. The inside of the store was almost finished. It was the opposite of Tea Time. Ford Essex had made a mighty effort to erase every bit of history from the building and replace it with all of the trappings of modernism. It was Silicon Valley on acid.

Ford Essex walked behind the stainless-steel counter. "A latte and a cappuccino. Am I right?" he asked.

"It's like you're a mind reader," Lucy gushed in full Scarlett O'Hara form. He turned around and flipped on the espresso machine.

"Ruth is going to kill him fifteen different ways," Lucy muttered to me.

"This is madness. Doesn't he know the dangers involved with this craziness?" I muttered back.

He handed us our coffee in paper to-go cups. "Taste that and tell me it's not the best coffee in the world."

I tasted it. It wasn't the best coffee in the world. Just like Ruth had said, it tasted of corporate evil, like the coffee had been delivered in the same box as the paper cups and plastic swizzle sticks. It was cold and anonymous, and it would probably make a fortune and put Ruth out of business.

"It's the best coffee in the world," I lied. "I thought the water main broke."

"Oh, that," he said and smiled slightly, which gave me chills up my body. "Sometimes I'm a playful man. I like to play. She started it, by the way. She called the cops on me because the crew started at seven this morning. But I've got to get this place up and running on Monday. I don't have time to dick around."

Lucy shot him another charming Southern comment,

which pleased him. We promised to be his most loyal customers, and he let us go with our coffees. Once outside, I threw it away.

"That man gives me a bad feeling," I told Lucy.

"Be nice, Gladie. He's breathing borrowed air."

Lucy drove us over to Bridget's townhouse to convince her to sneak away from tax season and have lunch with us. Our argument was going to be something like, "Everyone's got to eat, Bridget," and we planned a united front to bend her to our will to enjoy her company while we ate Cobb salads.

Lucy rang the doorbell when we arrived, and Bridget didn't answer. I could hear her clicking the keys on her computer through the door. I tried the doorknob, and it turned. Bridget must have forgotten to lock the door, and Lucy and I walked in.

Bridget was sitting at her dining room table with her laptop. She was drowning in mountains of paper. "What are you doing here?" she asked as she continued to type.

"We're kidnapping you, darlin'," Lucy told her. "Lunch with the girls."

Bridget pushed her hoot owl glasses on her nose. Her bright blue eye shadow practically glowed through the lenses, like it was signaling some kind of message. "Oh, that's right, the lunch," Bridget said and made a theatrical winking gesture to her. The hair on the back of my neck stood up.

"What's happening?" I asked. "What are you two up to?"

"We're kidnapping you," Bridget said and slapped her hand over her mouth. "Oh, darn it. I spilled the beans."

"You would be the worst spy," Lucy complained, pouting.

"I'm so confused. I thought we were kidnapping Bridget," I said.

"The romantic vacation," Lucy said. "You and Spencer. We want to know what happened."

"Did he ask you? Did he ask you?" Bridget asked, breathlessly, hopping up and down in her chair, her seven-month baby bump putting on an impressive show.

"Be careful, Bridget," I told her. "You're going to have Lech right here and now."

"I changed his name. The baby is now Delano."

"What kind of name is that?" Lucy asked. "A commie?"

"That's the middle name of our greatest president. Franklin Delano Roosevelt."

"It's a very nice name," I said, continuing with my strategy not to judge or criticize a mother. Parents were terrifying creatures. Even though there were a million ways to raise a child, I had learned in my life that every parent thinks their way is the best way, and it's best for an outsider to just agree with them. Lucy hadn't learned this lesson, however.

"What about Franklin? Isn't that better than Delano? Frank is a nice, normal name."

Uh oh. Lucy had used the "normal" word, which was a death sentence as far as Bridget was concerned. I didn't know why Lucy was making trouble. Delano was a hell of a lot better than Lech, which had been Bridget's previous name for her unborn child.

"What do you mean by normal?" Bridget asked, standing and rubbing her belly. "Do you mean misogynistic, patriarchal, racist, xenophobic? That kind of normal?"

Oh, geez. It had gotten ugly fast. Too many syllables were being flung around. I had to change the subject to something worse to steer the conversation away from bad baby names.

"Ask me what?" I asked. "What did who ask me what?"

But I understood what they wanted to know. Did Spencer ask me to marry him. Or at very least, did Spencer ask me to move into the house across the street, which I had been told he was interested in buying.

"We were only there for twenty minutes," I said.

"Talk about bad timing," Lucy said. "I love Zelda, but she's supposed to be making love matches, not breaking them up."

"Nobody broke anything up," I said.

"So, he asked you?" Bridget asked and burst into tears. She cried big, rolling sobs. "I'm so-so-so happy," she stuttered through her tears. "You two are perfect for each other. I don't normally believe in the patriarchal, transactional custom of buying a woman to put her in life-long servitude to a man and make her a brood-brood-brood mare. But in this case, it's so-so-so romantic." She barked out the last word, loudly and broke down into more sobs.

Hormones.

They're such a bitch.

"We need to get her food," Lucy told me.

"I need a hamburger," Bridget cried. "And French fries. Lots of them."

Bridget had gone from curiosity to excitement to anger to blubbering joy in three minutes. I thought she would at the very least need fries and would probably need a milkshake, too. Instead of going to our normal place, Saladz, we decided to drive to Burger Boy.

I had never actually eaten inside Burger Boy before. I had been purely drive thru takeout before, but now Bridget needed her burger fix, and the three us wanted to sit and dish the dirt. When we got our meals and sat down, Bridget and Lucy attacked me immediately for details.

"No proposal. Nothing about the house," I said.

"Damn it," Lucy replied, inspecting her hamburger.

"Was he about to ask you?" Bridget asked. "Preparing?"

"Well, we got there and starting doing boyfriend-girlfriend stuff in the shower, and that was when the dead girl showed up and pretty much stopped everything."

Lucy's hamburger fell out of her grip and landed with a splat onto her French fries.

"You were doing boyfriend-girlfriend stuff in the shower?" Bridget asked. "Weren't you afraid of slipping?"

"Forget that, darlin'," Lucy interrupted. "A dead girl showed up?"

"Oh, yeah. I guess I forgot about that."

"You forgot about a dead girl showing up?" Bridget asked, her eyes wide and her mouth agape. She and Lucy exchanged a what-the-hell look. "You're the death magnet, Gladie. You're Miss Marple. Normally, a dead girl showing up would get you all fired up. Obsessed." She put her elbow on the table and turned in to me, her face centimeters from mine. "Are you all right, Gladie? Is it Zelda? Was the event more than an event?"

"No," I said, but my voice croaked with the emotion that the memory brought up of the hotel and knowing somehow that something was wrong with my grandmother. It had turned out only to be an event. Ten days of rest while I took over the matchmaking. But obviously, it had turned me upside down because I hadn't given the murdered woman another thought. Instead, I had been thinking about Easter egg hunts.

"She was murdered," I said out loud.

Lucy put a fry into her mouth. "Wherever you go. It's amazing. I used to know a woman like you, but with her it was spiders. They were in her bed, her shoes, her cereal. Spiders everywhere like they were attracted to her. With you, it's murdered people."

She was totally right. Wherever I went, I stumbled on murdered people. "That's not true, Lucy," I said. "And Spencer was there, too. So, I only half stumbled on her. Spencer stumbled on the other half."

I gave them the rundown about the young woman with the ice bucket and then seeing her later in our bed, murdered. "And I passed out. When I woke up, the police were there, and that's when I felt Grandma."

"Felt?" Bridget asked.

"Saw. No, felt. No, saw. I don't know."

Lucy nodded and popped another fry into her mouth. "This is good."

"So you left to check on Zelda," Bridget said, placing her

hand on mine. She was such a good friend. Even though she judged society and traditions on a regular basis, she never judged me. Bridget was a safe space, a friend forever no matter what.

"Yes, and then there was the sumo wrestler and the Easter egg hunt committee."

Lucy nodded. "Scary."

"Scary," I agreed, but now my mind was full of the girl with the ice bucket, not matchmaking and town events. How did she get into our room? The door locked automatically, like all hotel rooms. And why was she murdered? And how? And then there was the question that always hooked me and made me go down a path of investigation: Why?

"Holy cow, she's got the look in her eye again, Bridget," Lucy said, pointing at my face with her finger, which was greasy from the French fries.

"Maybe she has gas," Bridget suggested, eyeing me.

I did have some gas, but I didn't think that was it. "I don't even know her name," I said, more to myself than to my friends. "A stranger, murdered and put in my bed. Or murdered in my bed. I don't know. I don't know anything." I had fallen down on the job. I had done a disservice to my Miss Marple sensibilities.

"I bet Spencer knows," Lucy said. "I bet he's got the whole police report, and he's been studying it."

"He's been watching a lot of Family Guy," I said. "The

murder wasn't in his jurisdiction."

I took a bite of my cheeseburger. I had gotten it with extra, special sauce, and it dripped onto my fries, which was a plus, as far as I was concerned.

"I need to find some time to go back to the hotel," I said with my mouth full.

"I've got lots of time. I'll go with you," Lucy said, excited.

"I can go with you next week," Bridget said. "After tax season is over."

Her phone rang, and she answered it. After saying, hello, she fell into concentration, and Lucy and I continued to talk about murder while we ate our lunch.

"Please," Bridget croaked after a moment. "Don't do this." She turned off her phone and turned her head away from us.

I put my hand on her back. "Bridget, what's wrong?"

She shook her head. "Nothing. Everything's fine."

Lucy shot me a look: *Danger, Will Robinson.* Bridget had been hormonal, so a marketing call could have set her off, but it could have been something bad, too.

"Bridget," I said and let my voice trail off. "Did the creation of the Bookkeepers of America Union fall through again?"

"No, I mean, yes, but that's not it," she said turning back

to us. She wiped a tear from her cheek.

"Is it Lech? I mean, Delano?" I asked. "Is the baby okay?"

I had gone with her to all of her doctor visits since she had gotten pregnant, and as far as I knew, her pregnancy was going without a hitch.

"No, not that," Bridget whispered, her voice hoarse from emotion. "It's him."

"Who?"

"Him. He's threatening to take Delano. He says he can get full custody, and I'll never see my child after he's born."

Tears streamed down her cheeks, and her glasses fogged up.

"Who's threatening you?" Lucy asked. "I don't understand."

But I understood. I knew who was threatening Bridget and her baby, even if I didn't know his identity.

"The father," Bridget said, her voice barely audible. "My baby's father."

CHAPTER 5

Love comes in many forms, split into categories with different names and attitudes toward it. But these are lies, dolly. Because love is love is love is love. There is no difference. If you have to quantify and qualify love, then it's not real. Because love is love, and your matches will know it when they feel it. If they feel it. But they'll come to you and ask: "Is this true love? Is it real? Can I trust it?" If they ask these questions, the answer is no. Because love is sure. The rest is kibbitzing.

Lesson 10, Matchmaking advice from your Grandma Zelda

Lucy and I plied Bridget with milkshakes and onion rings, but she wouldn't tell us who her baby's father was. I figured that he had to be somebody really bad, like a Columbian drug lord or a serial killer. All we knew was that the guy had been a one-shot deal, and Bridget had kept her pregnancy a secret from him. But somehow, he found out, and he was coming after her with a vengeance. Bridget assured us that she would take care of it and not to worry.

But I was worried. Lucy took her home, and I promised myself to ask Spencer to help Bridget.

"I don't know what we're supposed to do first," Lucy said as she stopped her car in front of my house. "Do we start investigating the murder of the ice bucket woman, or do we get the thumbscrews out for Bridget's mysterious baby daddy?"

Since Bridget was my best friend, there really wasn't a choice. She was my priority. But she didn't want me to be involved. She didn't even want to tell me who the father was. "Let me talk to Spencer about it," I told Lucy. "I'll call you tomorrow."

"We could get Harry to help, you know, if we can't fix it the normal way." Harry was more or less in retirement, but he had made his living in suspicious ways. I figured his way of fixing it had something to do with a broken nose and two broken legs, which I wasn't totally opposed to if it would save Bridget, but that would be the last resort.

I walked up the driveway and reached the door as a group of people were leaving. "We're never going to get this done," Josephine from the Easter egg hunt committee complained to me as she passed. Her face was a sheen of sweat, and she looked like she had just been defeated in battle. "Do you know how many five-hundred-one-thousand eggs are?"

I didn't know how to answer that so I shook my head.

"It's a shit ton of eggs, that's how many!" she shrieked.

"Shut up, Josephine," a short, wide man said, walking around her. He was bulky with muscles instead of fat, but he was almost as wide as he was tall. Another middle-aged member of the committee, I assumed, and he was pissed off, too.

"You shut up," Josephine said. "Just because you're the chair. Well, I'm the co-chair."

"I know. You never let me forget it. But we're doing this. World record. Stop trying to put the kibosh on it with your negative energy."

She pursed her lips at him and rolled her eyes. "Negative energy. Oh, please."

I walked inside and was hit with an overpowering wave of hard-boiled egg stink. I pinched my nose. "Didn't anyone think to open a window?" I shouted into the house.

Spencer stuck his head out of the kitchen. "Every window is open, Pinky. Help, me. I'm in hell."

I put my purse down and walked into the kitchen. There were four large pots on the stove, each filled and furiously boiling eggs.

"I thought you were with Harry," I said.

Spencer hugged me tight against him. "They drafted me, Pinky. They wouldn't let me leave. I've been boiling eggs for hours.

It's my personal Vietnam. I think I have PTSD already."

"You smell nice," he added, nuzzling my neck.

"I thought you had PTSD."

He squeezed my butt. "I know of a good therapy."

"What about the eggs?"

"What about *my* eggs, Pinky? What about *my* eggs? I've got blue eggs. You know what I mean?"

"We have sex about five times a week."

"Exactly. We only have sex about five times a week."

"You sound like you're begging for sex."

"It's the new me. The sensitive Spencer. Begging instead of demanding."

I didn't know about the sensitive Spencer. I kind of liked the Neanderthal, frat boy, dirty-minded Spencer.

"No comment on the sensitive Spencer?" he asked as he nibbled at my earlobe. "I love that you don't smell like hard-boiled eggs."

"What do I smell like?" I breathed, bending my neck to the side to give him more access for his lips.

"Like you want me."

"That might be the French fries. I ate the Jumbo Burger Boy Special."

He picked me up, and I wrapped my legs around him. Placing me on the counter, he kissed me for real. The begging, sensitive Spencer was long gone, and the demanding, Neanderthal Spencer was back. He even pulled my hair a little, just to prove that he was all caveman and no amount of Phil Donahue. It worked. I squeezed him tighter with my legs, as if I was going in for the kill at a professional wrestling match. My tongue shot into his mouth, as if I was an ears, nose, and throat doctor checking his tonsils.

His tonsils were good.

Very, very good.

Zing! Zow! Whoa...whoa...momma! We were the superhero comics of sex, and we hadn't even gotten past first base. But first base with Spencer was the height of erotica. I was burning up, with arousal throbbing between my legs, and my eyes had rolled back in my head. Spencer ground his erection against my jeans. Damned, stupid jeans. Naked would have been so much better. Why wasn't I naked? How could I have been so stupid to wear clothes?

As if he read my mind, he popped open my jeans and unzipped them, slipping his hand down. At any moment, someone could have walked in to see Spencer with his giant erection pressing against his pants and his hand in my pants, going to town. But frankly, I didn't care who walked in, or at least I didn't give it one thought, let alone a second thought. My focus wasn't even on my gorgeous boyfriend or his talented fingers. Instead my focus was entirely on the orgasm that was almost, almost, almost there. I was on the bridge of ecstasy that ended in the tightening deep inside me, and ended violently, making me dig my fingernails into Spencer's back and making me bite his shoulder to quiet the scream that erupted from my throat with the last gasp of fulfillment.

It was like a green light went on for Spencer. He let his pants drop to his ankles, and he replaced his hand, burying himself deep inside me. He went from zero to a hundred miles an hour in a couple seconds. It was the opposite of tantric sex. It was drive-in, back of the car, hurry up the cops are coming, sex. He pounded into me, almost showing off his cardio fitness. But it was interval training, not a marathon, and it was over fast. Within a matter of minutes, we were holding each other, worn out and dripping with sweat and completely sated.

"Woman, you turn me inside out," he said.

"Is that good or bad?"

"I never thought it could be like this. Do I sound like a romance novel?"

"I'm not a big reader."

"I wonder if Vin Diesel ever said that. 'I never thought it could be like this.' It's possible."

A timer dinged, and Spencer let me go. "My eggs are done," he announced, happily. Our ride on the counter seemed to lift his spirits. He put his pants back on and turned off the stove.

"I'm going to check on Grandma and take a quick shower," I told him, as he poured the hot water into the sink. "You okay here?"

"I'm never going to eat eggs, again. Never. Fuck omelets."

"I'll take that as a yes," I said and walked upstairs.

I felt a little guilty, leaving Spencer to deal with the hard-boiled eggs. After all, I had been the one to give the go ahead for the world record, and I hadn't boiled one egg.

I walked into my grandmother's room. She was sitting up in bed, watching a Cary Grant movie on Spencer's television. Meryl had left, and she was alone, but she seemed happy, and her color was good.

"Hello, dolly. How were the girls?"

"Bridget has some trouble."

"That's going to be difficult to work out," she told me, muting the TV.

I sat down on the chair next to her bed. "I'm worried about her. It's not like her to keep secrets."

"Secrets are a cancer, but we're all afflicted, bubbeleh. There's a storm brewing," she added, looking toward the window.

"A real one, or a Bridget one?"

"Both. And more." She closed her eyes. I stopped

breathing while I watched her. I worried that she wasn't feeling well, that her event was turning into something worse. But her breathing was strong and steady, and she didn't seem uncomfortable. So, it was something else that made her close her eyes.

Focus. She was focusing.

After a couple of minutes, her eyes opened, and she patted the space on the bed next to her. I sat on the bed, and she took my hand, giving it a squeeze.

"You're a strong woman, Gladie. Do you believe that?"

No, I didn't believe it at all.

"You're a strong woman," she repeated, not waiting for me to answer. "The people you love will need your strength."

"You? You need my strength?" I asked, holding back the tears that threatened to fall.

"I'm a strong woman, too," she said, smiling at me. "Don't worry about me, dolly. I'm here, safe from the storm. But it's coming, and it's a bad one. Dangerous. Very dangerous."

My heart pounded in my chest, and it was hard to breathe. "What should I do? How can I handle the storm?"

"Don't trust anyone."

Spencer and I ate dinner with my grandmother in her room, and she went to sleep early. When we went to bed, Spencer pulled me in close and sighed.

"Maybe I should buy a new television," he said.

"It's only for ten days." But I had gotten used to watching TV in bed, too.

"But it's baseball season, and there's a new Smart TV out. The high def is so high that it's like the players are in the room. You think there's room for a sixty-inch in here?"

"That's what she said," I said and giggled.

"You are five years old," he teased, using my words against me.

"You know what? I didn't have coffee today. Just a couple sips from the new coffee place next to Ruth's."

"That guy must have a death wish," Spencer said. "First rule of living in Cannes is to not cross Ruth Fletcher."

"Thank you for helping with the eggs," I said. "Sorry you got drafted."

Spencer kissed the top of my head. "This has been some vacation. Not exactly what I had planned. But at least I'm not on the job. I got a call about a couch running over one of my patrolmen. I'm glad I missed that one."

"Me, too," I said, hoping he wouldn't find out that I had been responsible for that. It was time to ask him about Bridget and about the woman with the ice bucket, but I didn't know how to start. He didn't like me getting involved in murder investigations, but if we started with Bridget, we would never get to the murder.

"I'm worried about Bridget," I said, softly.

"Is the baby okay? Do you want me to take you over there?"

"The baby's fine. But the father of the baby is making himself known, and he's threatening Bridget, saying he's going to get custody."

Spencer pulled back and looked at me. "Who's the father?"

"I don't know. I'm guessing it's either Hitler or Mussolini, because she won't cough up the name or any information about him. I suppose he found out about the baby, and he's mad and wants to punish her."

"Well, he deserved to know about the baby."

"I trust Bridget to be smart. If she thought he shouldn't know, then he shouldn't know."

"The law's the law," Spencer said, making me furious. "He has a right to fifty-percent custody."

I moved away from him in bed. "Why are you taking Hitler's side against Bridget?"

"You don't know he's Hitler."

"If Bridget says he's Hitler, then he's Hitler."

"Did Bridget say he's Hitler?"

"What does that have to do with anything? Bridget is scared and worried! How dare you? How dare you!"

I turned away from him and punched my pillow.

"Does this mean we're not going to play airline pilot and flight attendant tonight?"

"No," I growled. "You've been grounded."

"But Pinky…"

"Don't but Pinky me. You took Hitler's side over my best friend. Traitor. I hope the Padres lose every game this season."

I didn't fall asleep until four in the morning. Then, I dreamed that there was a storm in my bedroom. I was soaking wet, and the wind was whipping me when Hitler burst through the door and stole my ultra high definition television. I ran after him, but Bridget stopped me and warned me that if I continued to chase him, I would never drink another cup of coffee again.

I woke up in a sweat at four-thirty. I had slept for a measly thirty minutes. Spencer was dead to the world. I rolled out of bed, slipped on a pair of jeans, a pair of Spencer's socks, one of his cotton sweaters, and my Keds. After pulling my hair back into a ponytail, I checked on my grandmother. She was already up and watching Katharine Hepburn on the classic movie channel.

"You want breakfast?" I whispered her way.

"Meryl will be here in an hour with chicken and waffles," she said. "Go ahead and get your coffee at Ruth's."

"Is Tea Time open this early?"

"It is this morning."

I thought about trying to go back to sleep, but after my fight with Spencer and my nightmare, I knew I wouldn't be able to. I grabbed my wallet out of my purse, put my coat on, and left the house, closing the door quietly behind me.

The air at four-thirty in the morning in the mountains was cold and crisp, but it smelled faintly of eggs. The sky was lit with stars, like they were painted on with large brushes. Nobody was around. The house across the street was covered in dark blue tarps, spooky and a reminder of possibilities with Spencer.

Our fight didn't leave me angry at him, but I had been surprised that he hadn't helped me help Bridget, and that he would defend an anonymous man over my best friend. Wasn't a boyfriend—a boyfriend who may or may not be ready to buy a house for me and possibly more—supposed to be supportive, no matter what?

Boy, I needed coffee.

Main Street was mostly dark, except for Tea Time. I tried the door, but it was locked, so I knocked hard. After a couple of minutes, Ruth answered.

"What the hell?" she asked, looking me up and down with her Louisville Slugger clutched tightly in her hand. "I thought you were the jerk from next door. I almost homered your head, Gladie."

"I need coffee. I need lots of coffee."

"Come on in." She let me in and looked both ways down the street before she closed the door. Tea Time smelled like freshly baked pastries.

"Did you make scones?"

"Sit down. I got ten minutes, so I'll eat with you."

She gave me a latte in a large mug, and she put a teapot on the table, along with a plate of scones, a bowl of jam, and a bowl of clotted cream. My mouth watered.

"Gee, thanks, Ruth," I gushed.

"So, why are you up this early?" she asked, smearing cream onto a scone. "Where's the cop? If he was in my bed, I wouldn't be wandering the town in the middle of the night."

She had a point. I should have been in bed, enjoying my muscly man with perfect bone structure. "Oh, please, Ruth. I'm a modern woman. I have matches to make and an Easter egg hunt to help organize."

She pointed at me and chewed. "Is that thing your fault?"

"Of course not," I lied.

"Every pot in this town is filled with eggs. They're shipping eggs in from Sacramento, I hear. I guess they got a lot of chickens, there. It's a madhouse in town. They wanted to use my kitchen. I put a stop to that, let me tell you."

I took a sip of the latte. So good. So, so, so, good. I moaned with pleasure. "You make the best coffee, Ruth. Not like the jerk next door."

Ruth dropped her scone onto her plate. "You drank his coffee? You went into that antiseptic, sterile, corporate hellscape next door?"

"No," I lied. She arched an eyebrow and scowled. She could read me like a book. "Well, just for a minute. He made me. And Lucy made me. I took one sip of the coffee and threw it away. I'll never go in there again, Ruth! I promise! I promise! Don't homer my head!"

Yes, I was scared of Ruth. Even though she was ancient and didn't have a working joint anywhere on her body, I had no doubts she could take me in a fight. Because she was ornery as hell.

I took another sip of my latte, and moaned again. "You make the best coffee," I told her, again, truthfully. She picked up her scone and took a bite.

"Can you believe that the jerk opened a coffee place next door to my tea shop?" she asked. "Coffee? And the name of the place? Buckstars? Who does he think he's going to fool with that cockamamie name? Buckstars. Buckstars. Buckstars."

She was like a broken record. Or like an old woman who was probably going to be run out of business by a jerk with a name ripped off from Starbucks.

"Great scones," I told her, taking a bite and washing it down with my latte.

"Mr. Jerk is going to have his toilet back up," Ruth told me, as she poured herself a cup of tea.

"He is?"

"Yep."

"You're going to go full on commando on his ass, aren't you, Ruth?"

"I'm more commando than John Wayne, Gladie. He has no idea what's coming."

I thought about that for a moment. "Grandma said something about a storm coming."

"That woman's elevator doesn't go to the top floor. I swear her rectum has got some real talent, 'cause she talks out of her ass more than anyone I've ever met. I checked the forecast this morning. No sign of rain for the next ten days."

I hoped she was right. I hoped my grandmother had been talking out of her ass and that there was no reason for me to be strong. I never wanted to be strong. I wanted to be weak and whiny and perfectly happy.

"May I have another latte?" I asked Ruth.

I ate three scones and drank two lattes, thinking about all the things I had to worry about while I got my fill of sugar and caffeine. People started to file in at around five, old people who started their day before the sun and ate the Early Bird Special for dinner every night. I recognized most of them, and they all smelled of hard-boiled eggs.

"Zelda's granddaughter!" one of them called. "Zelda's granddaughter! Do you know when the shipment from Sacramento is coming in? We've already cleaned out Walley's. We've got to boil the eggs, paint the eggs, and hide the eggs. We've only got one week."

All of the geezers stared at me, as if I was in charge and knew anything about organizing town events. "It's coming in any time now," I said, plastering a smile on my face. "Oodles of eggs."

"Oodles?" one of the early birds asked me.

"And gobs," I added, winking at him and shooting him

with my index finger.

I put five dollars on the table and backed out of Tea Time. "Keep up the good work!" I yelled, waving like I was leaving on a transatlantic luxury cruise in the 1930s. "The town will thank you for all of your hard egg work!"

"Lord, girl, get out while you can," Ruth grumbled while she poured tea.

I gave one last wave, and I opened the door and stepped out into the street. Taking a deep, healing breath, I looked around for more townsfolk who wanted me to tell them what to do. Nope, I was safe. It was just me and the sunrise. I should have a clear shot to home. Next door to Tea Time, Ford Essex had put out a sign. "Buy one cappuccino, get three for free," it read. Uh oh. Ruth was doomed. She was beloved in town, but so was hard-earned cash.

I looked both ways and jogged across the street.

I jumped a foot in the air when a siren rang out in the quiet early morning.

Sonofabitch.

A police car screeched to a stop by me as I reached the sidewalk on the other side of the street. I looked around for an escape, but there was no way I could outrun a police car, or in this case, Terri's gun, because she was getting out of the car, and she was pointing her gun right at me.

I gulped and put my hands up.

"Good morning, Terri," I said. "Beautiful morning, isn't it? Early bird gets the worm, I always say." Actually, I had never said that. I didn't care about worms, and I definitely wasn't a morning person.

Terri walked with a slight limp, which I assumed had something to do with being run down by a runaway couch. She kept her gun aimed at my face.

I kept my smile on my face. Sure, I didn't think she would ever like me, but I couldn't figure out another strategy to get her to stop harassing me. "How can I help you? There's some delicious fresh scones at Tea Time if you have a five-minute breakfast break."

"You jaywalked."

"I did?"

"You jaywalked right in front of me. You're a danger to the public safety. Laws are there for a reason, you know."

"You're right. You're right. Of course, there are no traffic lights in the Historic District, soooo…"

"Are you resisting arrest?" she asked, squinting at me.

"Am I getting arrested?"

She waved her gun at me, like she was trying to decide which part of my face to shoot off first. "I guess I can't arrest you, but you're getting a citation. No sudden movements!"

I nodded. "No sudden movements."

To my relief, she holstered her gun. To my consternation, she pulled out her ticket book and started writing. I sighed while I kept my hands up. At this rate, I would have ten thousand dollars in tickets. At some point, I would have to show them to Spencer and try to get them taken care of, but I knew that he would blame me for antagonizing Terri.

Damned Spencer. First Hitler and now Terri. Where were his priorities?

"Jaywalking," Terri said, ripping off a ticket and handing it to me. Then, she kept writing. "Annoying the morning," she said, handing me another one.

"Annoying the morning? Is that a thing?"

Terri lifted her gorgeous head, stared at me with her gorgeous eyes, and flipped her gorgeous hair. "It is with you. You. Are. Annoying."

Served me right to wake up early. I would never do it again.

"Fine. I'm annoying," I said, putting my hand out to get my second ticket of the morning.

But she didn't give it to me. She was distracted by a car driving down the street at a snail's pace, swerving from side to side.

"A drunk driver at five in the morning. What's this world coming to?" she asked, staring at the car. At least it wasn't a couch. So, it was just normal police stuff.

"People are so irresponsible," I agreed, trying to get on her good side.

"Don't move. I'm not done with you," she ordered and went into her car and turned the siren on. The meandering car slowed and ran up on the sidewalk in front of the pharmacy. The driver opened her window and stuck her head out.

"Leave me alone! I'm on my way to work!" Then, she hiccoughed, and I got a whiff of the booze on her breath from half a block away. It was Merry Ferry. She worked in the orchards, doing something with manure. I wasn't sure what because I didn't know a thing about agriculture. But I did know that she was one of my grandmother's unmatchables, a person she had tried to match more than ten times without any luck. Grandma liked to say there was an ass for every seat and a hat for every head, but it didn't look like there was a love match for Merry Ferry, and maybe that's why she was so aggressive about being pulled over.

"Turn off your motor!" Terri barked over her loudspeaker. She was waking up the town, and people were coming out of buildings to see what the hubbub was about.

"I have trees to take care of!" Merry shouted at her. "What's the matter with you? Don't you like trees?"

"Turn off your motor, or I'll shoot you!"

Terri was a real winner. At this rate, she was going to shoot up the whole town. I felt a duty to Merry and Cannes to diffuse the situation. And I wasn't giving up on getting Terri to like me, either.

"Don't worry, Terri. I know her. I'll get her to listen," I told her and walked toward Merry's car.

"Freeze!" Terri shouted at me.

"Don't worry, Terri. I'm glad to help," I told her smiling at her.

When I got to Merry's car, she blinked at me, as if she was trying to focus, and she probably was. "Is that you, Gladie? Zelda's granddaughter?"

"Yep, it's me. How are you doing?"

"You know. Same ole. Same ole. I mean, besides the egg thing. I hard-boiled four dozen eggs last night."

"Hey, thanks a lot," I said, surprised. It was nice to see the entire community coming together for the egg hunt.

"I told you to turn off your motor," Terri yelled, walking up to the car. "And I told you to mind your own business!" she yelled at me.

"It's not a problem, Terri. I love to help. This is Merry. Hey Merry, would you turn off your car?"

Merry turned it off, and I threw Terri an I-told-you-so look. Terri gave me a shove, and she bent over and got into Merry's face.

"You've been drinking," she barked at Merry. "You're driving drunk."

"No, I'm not," Merry insisted. "The cocaine totally sobered me."

It wasn't a good start.

"Get out of the car," Terri shouted.

"I can't. I have to get to work."

"Get out of the car!"

"Merry, I think you have to get out of the car," I said, gently.

"Stay out of this!" Terri yelled at me.

"Don't be mean to Gladie!" Merry yelled. "Gladie's nice. Gladie doesn't care if I drink Jack Daniels before I drive to work."

"Oh, is that so?" Terri asked, looking at me, as if I had shoved the whiskey bottle in Merry's face this morning.

"No! I mean, I would never tell anyone to disobey the law," I insisted.

"Get out of the car," Terri shouted. Her beautiful face was bright red and splotchy. She was furious.

"Merry," I started.

"Stay out of it!" Terri shouted and gave me a strong shove that sent me flying against the door to the pharmacy.

"Police brutality!" Merry yelled. "Attica! Attica!"

"Shut up," Terri said and touched Merry's arm.

And then it happened. In a speed of light, Merry bent over and clamped her teeth into Terri's forearm. Like a pitbull, her jaw locked and no amount of tugging, slapping, or screaming by Terri would get Merry to let go.

Across the street, Ruth was standing outside of Tea Time, shaking her head at me, as if it were my teeth sinking into Terri's flesh. She had a point. I should have stayed out of it, like Terri commanded, and now for the second time in two days, I had escalated a traffic stop until Terri was injured.

She probably didn't like me any better, and now I would be doomed to a series of new tickets. Somehow, I would have to fix the situation.

But not now. Now, Merry was still biting Terri, and Terri was screaming, her voice so high-pitched that I thought it could break glass.

"I guess my work here is done," I muttered and walked past them toward home.

CHAPTER 6

What's the perfect age to get married? I hear that debate a lot. Some say older because it takes a certain maturity to be married. Some say younger when a person isn't stuck in their ways, yet. So, what do I say? I say, when you're ready, you're ready.

Lesson 52, Matchmaking advice from your Grandma Zelda

I turned onto my grandmother's street and was surprised to see Spencer standing in front of the house across from Grandma's house. He was talking to a man who was wearing a tool belt and holding a tablet, pointing at different places on the tarp-covered house. I stopped in my tracks, scared to go on. Spencer froze, too, and as if he sensed me, turned and looked my way.

He shrugged his shoulders and smirked. I melted, and our

fight disappeared from my memory. Spencer was wearing jeans and a white t-shirt. His hands were hooked in his pockets, he was barefoot, and his hair was mussed. He was the sexiest man on the planet. He would make ice melt. I walked to him.

"Gladie, this is Urijah," Spencer said. I shook the man's hand.

"Thank you for trusting me with your house," he said. "I can't wait to get started."

"You're welcome?" I said like a question. My house? Did I have a house? I felt Spencer's eyes on me, but I didn't dare look at him.

"We can start tomorrow and be done by the beginning of July."

July. The house would be done in July. I didn't know what that meant or what it had to do with me. Spencer and I were overdue for a serious discussion.

Spencer reached out and put his hand around my waist. "Sounds perfect, Urijah," he said.

"Cleanup is going to take a while, and then we can sit down and go over specifics. Are you going to use the interior designer we talked about?" Urijah asked.

"We're going to talk about that," Spencer said.

We were going to talk about an interior designer? Was I in

the Twilight Zone? I had never had an interior designer. I had never even had an interior before.

My heart pounded in my chest, but I definitely should have had a third latte because I thought I might be dreaming. Spencer and Urijah talked about retaining walls, drywall, and other kinds of walls while I drifted.

I drifted far away from thoughts of houses and commitment and even past thoughts of Spencer and his naked body. My brain moved on to safe things to think about, like Bridget's problems and the mysterious murdered girl in the hotel room.

And Oreos. I was having lots of thoughts about Oreos.

Spencer walked home with me after the contractor left, and we didn't say a word about "my house."

"Clear your schedule tomorrow so I can take you out for dinner," Spencer said, as we walked up the driveway.

"You're taking me out to dinner?"

"Yep."

"But Grandma. But the eggs."

"Tomorrow for dinner, Pinky. Six o'clock just like regular people. Dress in that little red dress you have. You don't have to wear underwear, in case you were wondering."

"Gee, thanks," I said.

He pulled me close and looked deep into my eyes, taking my breath away. "I love you, Gladie Burger."

"Why?"

"Shit if I know."

I loved him, too, but I felt out of control and overwhelmed, like my life was two steps ahead of me at all times since the first time Spencer had kissed me. I was disoriented, unbalanced, freaking out.

"Who killed the woman with the ice bucket?" I asked.

Spencer smirked his little smirk. "I've been wondering when you would get around to that. I thought you were broken."

"Just distracted. Who was she?"

"Mamie Foster. She was on vacation with her new husband. He's been arrested. They found the murder weapon in his shaving kit."

"They found the murderer?" I asked, disappointed. That had been the first time that had happened. Normally, it was a mystery, and I would butt in and solve it.

"Disappointed, Miss Marple?" Spencer asked.

"Of course not," I lied.

He opened the door, and waited for me to walk in. "Although, it's a little too pat, a little too neat, finding the murder weapon in the husband's shaving kit."

Spencer closed the door behind us. "Pinky, don't start."

"I mean, why would he hide the murder weapon where it would definitely be found? Why didn't he toss it somewhere?"

"Maybe a man who kills his wife on his honeymoon isn't thinking too clearly, Pinky. Most killers aren't criminal masterminds, you know."

"And why would he kill her in our bed?" I asked, walking to the kitchen. Spencer followed me.

"Again, not a genius. Not thinking clearly."

I put the coffee pot on for Grandma. It was almost seven, and she probably wanted a cup. "Let's think about this a moment. We saw her. She had an ice bucket and was happy, skipping down the hallway. So, what happened? Her husband got a sudden mood swing and ran after her in the ice room and then chased her into our locked room, where he killed her? Did anyone check the ice room for clues?"

I cut a bagel in half and put it in the toaster. Spencer was leaning against the counter with his arms crossed. His mouth was open slightly and his eyes weren't blinking. "I'm sure law enforcement has done its job," he said finally, but he didn't sound totally convinced.

The toaster dinged, and I put the bagel on a plate. "You're probably right." But while I smeared cream cheese on the bagel, all

I was thinking about was how to find the time to get back to the hotel and check out the scene of the crime. I also needed to talk to the husband.

"You have that look on your face again," Spencer told me, handing me a coffee mug. I poured coffee into it and added sugar and milk.

"What was the murder weapon?" I asked him.

"A steak knife."

"Did they have room service? A steak dinner?"

Spencer and I locked eyes. "Pinky…" he said, like he was a car changing gears. It was all the answer I needed. No steak dinner. No reason that he would have had a steak knife.

I put the food and the coffee on a tray and picked it up, shrugging at Spencer. "I'm sure that law enforcement is doing what it's supposed to," I said and rolled my eyes.

Spencer's phone rang, and he answered it. "I'm on vacation," he said after a few seconds. I walked upstairs, and he followed me as he talked on the phone. "I don't care if she got bitten. I've gotten bitten more times on the job than anyone in California. Tell her to get a rabies shot and a tetanus shot and stop complaining. What? Say that again. Well, fine, so she only needs a tetanus shot. I don't think Merry has rabies."

He clicked off the phone. "Merry Ferry bit one of my cops."

"Really? That's weird."

At some point, Spencer was going to get wind about the terror that I had been inflicting on Terri, and boy was he going to give me hell, but I was hoping that I could win her over before that happened.

I knocked on my grandmother's door, and she told me to come in. I found her sitting on the chair next to her bed, and she was freshly showered and wearing her blue housedress and click-clack plastic slippers. From the sound of it, Meryl was in the bathroom. The television was on to a Claudette Colbert movie, and I caught Spencer looking longingly at his TV.

"You better get ready for the egg people, dolly," my grandmother told me as I put the tray down on her nightstand. "They're on their way, and they're panicking."

"Uh oh," I said, took my bagel, and ran out of the room. Spencer ran out, too.

"I'm out of here before they arrive," he said, as I stripped down and turned on the shower. "I'm running to Harry's. I never want to see an egg again."

"Okay, save yourself. I'll take one for the team." I took a thirty-second shower and braided my wet hair. I swiped some mascara on and dressed in slacks and a pink t-shirt. I checked on my grandmother to see if she needed anything. But she didn't need me. Grandma was back in bed, and Meryl was sitting on the chair. The television was blaring the CBS Sunday Morning show. And, oh yeah, there was a parrot sitting on Meryl's shoulder.

"Meryl, you have a bird sitting on your shoulder," I said.

"Gladie, it's a tragedy. Ishmael disappeared two years ago, and he came back this morning. He just flew through my kitchen window like nothing had happened," Meryl explained.

"And you didn't want him to come back?"

"Not like this! Not like this!"

I looked at my grandmother. "Meryl's bird came back changed, dolly."

The parrot looked like a normal parrot to me: Green. Feathers. A beak.

Then, the bird started to talk, but I didn't understand one word. "See?" Meryl said. "When he left, he spoke English. Now, I have no idea what he's saying."

"What language is that?" I asked.

"No idea," Meryl said.

"No idea," my grandmother repeated.

I heard the door open and shut downstairs. I didn't have time to worry about a bird who had left the country for two years or had taken some kind of intensive Berlitz course. "I'm sorry for your loss," I told Meryl, handed her my bagel, and went downstairs.

Josephine was setting up the chairs in the parlor. She had

brought a coffee cake, and I went to the kitchen to get the coffee pot and plates for the cake. "You're staying for the meeting, right?" Josephine asked me, walking into the kitchen. I nodded. "Because Cannes is going to be ground zero for World War Three. This egg thing has already made people psychotic. I know one woman who hasn't slept for twenty-four hours. She just keeps boiling eggs and repeats 'Eggs, eggs, eggs' over and over."

I hadn't boiled one egg, yet, and I was feeling guilty about it. "How many eggs have they boiled so far?"

"Fifty thousand. We're never going to make it."

By the time that I brought the coffee into the parlor, it had filled up with ten committee members and the two co-chairs. There was a lot of talk about how impossible it would be to prepare five-hundred-and-one thousand eggs within one week. And it wasn't just boiling. The eggs had to be dyed and hid.

"I was up all night, making the egg map," Griffin, the co-chair, announced, holding up a giant map, drawn onto brown butcher paper. He laid it out on the coffee table after we cleared away the cake and coffee. It was a crude representation of Cannes with little X's marked in red all over it.

"We're going to hide eggs in the orchards?" one of the committee members asked. "Normally, we only hide eggs in the Historic District. Actually, just the park."

"It's over five-hundred-thousand eggs," Griffin said, as if that explained it all.

Josephine studied the map. "You've got eggs on the roof of the pharmacy."

"Pretty much every roof. Kids are going to be falling off roofs like it's raining children," someone pointed out.

"Again, it's over five hundred thousand eggs," Griffin said.

"The gas station? The lake? How does that work with the lake?"

Griffin whipped the butcher paper off the coffee table and ripped it in two. "Everyone's a critic! Fine! You find five-hundred-and-one-thousand places to hide a goddamned egg!"

At this point in the breakdown of any town meeting, my grandmother would calm the masses and force everyone to make nice. Since I was her replacement, it was my job to turn down the tension. How could I do that? Xanax would work, but the only person I knew with Xanax was Lucy, and she wasn't there. And how could I force feed a group of elderly townsfolk to consume Xanax? I mulled it over, trying to figure out what elderly people did to relax. Buffets were good. And knitting. Actually, wasn't all of the Greatest Generation booze hounds? Didn't they like to drink sidecars and gimlets?

What the hell was a gimlet?

What the hell was a sidecar?

Oh, geez, I was out of ideas.

Griffin continued to rip the map into tiny pieces. Josephine was standing, screeching, and throwing her hands up. Various other committee members complained to each other that this was the dumbest thing the town had ever done.

That was saying a lot.

Xanax or no Xanax, I had to tamper this down in hurry. I stood up. "Now, now," I said. Nobody paid attention to me. It was like I was invisible. "Now, now!" I yelled.

"Hiding eggs in the lake?" Josephine shrieked. "Are we giving the kids diving gear to hunt for eggs this year?" She swung around, wildly, and caught me with her bony knuckles right on my chin. I flew back and hit my head on the wall and then crashed down onto the floor.

Lying flat on my back, I tried to catch my breath. Cannes's high society, meanwhile, leaned over me, giving me a good look at their droopy faces and what was left of their molars. "Why did you do that?" Josephine demanded. "You threw yourself in front of my hand. You practically broke it."

"I'm sorry," I said. With the group finally quiet and not fighting, I took my chance to get control over the meeting. "Can't we all be friends? We're trying to accomplish something meaningful for our town, something to be proud of. Sure, it's hard, but it's worthwhile."

I had no idea what I was talking about. It was a stupid Easter egg hunt. Kids went around, looking for colored, hard-boiled eggs. Who cared?

"She's right," Griffin said, looking down at me. "This is the biggest thing we've done in years. If we can't do it, nobody can."

"I agree," Josephine said and shook his hand.

We had turned a corner. Someone helped me up, and the committee was reinvigorated with the challenge before them. The committee broke up into smaller groups. One worked on the logistics for boiling the eggs, another for the dyeing, and the last about the hunt itself. I wandered among the small groups, nodding, like I knew what they were doing. They never drafted me for a specific task, which was a plus. I just had to look like I was busy, and like that, I never actually needed to be busy.

"You're the murder girl, right?" one of the committee members asked me. It was Alice, a widow with an unusual amount of chin hairs. She only had three, but they were at least two inches long. Thick and black. It was hard to pay attention to anything except for her chin hairs when she spoke to me. She was part of the dyeing group, and she had suggested that the eggs be painted in three colors, patriotic red, white, and blue.

"I've seen a couple murdered people. No more than the average person," I said.

"Are you kidding? The way I heard it you've stumbled, tripped, and fallen over a good dozen of them. I've never seen one murdered person. I've never even seen a murdered cat, and cats are murdered every day."

"They are?"

She nodded, and I watched her chin hairs move with her head. "It's mass murder out there for cats. Everyone knows that."

I didn't know that. "Oh, sure," I said.

"I would never kill a cat, but it wouldn't take much for me to kill a person," she continued, smiling. She looked into space, as if she was visualizing herself murdering some good for nothing human. "I could do it, easily," she explained. My arms sprouted goosebumps, and the hair on the back of my neck stood up. "Look at these muscles," she said, flexing her arm. Sure enough, she had a big bicep. "That's from seventy-five years of making homemade bread. So, I'd beat a man with my rolling pin. That would get him good. I probably could do it with one whack." She blinked. "Or I could stab him to death. I have a great knife set."

Josephine moved closer to me and whispered in my ear. "I saw a murdered person once in a very weird place. But I never told anyone. I can't tell you about it, but trust me, I know how you feel."

I moved on to the map group. They had started a new map and decided to ask the local businesses to hide eggs inside so that they wouldn't have to hide eggs on roofs or in the lake. "It's looking good," Griffin told me, taking a sip from a mug. "Great coffee by the way. Have you tried Buckstars, yet? I went in, and they gave me a Caramel Buckstarsiato a day before their grand opening. It was okay. But I wanted to go in and see the drama."

At first I thought he was talking about the war between Ruth and Buckstars. But the gleam in Griffin's eye was about something bigger.

"What drama?" my nosy self asked.

"I'm not one for gossip," he said, and the map group leaned forward to get an earful of Griffin not gossiping. "There's been some fooling around and cheating happening with those Buckstars owners. Kinky, scary stuff. Like that book that everyone bought, but with older people and not as much money."

"Fifty Shades book," one of the map group members supplied. "Best book I've ever read."

"What about you? You like that book?" Griffin asked me, winking.

"I need to check on the boil group," I said, moving away from Griffin.

Luckily, the doorbell rang at that moment, and I went to answer it. "You Zelda's girl?" a man asked me. He was wearing a jumpsuit with *Pete's Pesticides* written in red on his chest.

"I'm her granddaughter, Gladie."

He put his hand out, and I shook it. "I'm Bruce. Bruce Coyle. You're supposed to find me my soulmate."

I started to sweat. Big rolling beads of sweat popped out of my pores and instantly drenched me from my head to my toes. I would never be comfortable with the pressure of matchmaking. I wasn't good with commitment or responsibility, and the idea that I was responsible for another's lifetime of happiness or misery choked me and made me perspire.

But this was me, my career, and supposedly I had the gift. "Of course, Bruce. Come on in," I said and wiped my forehead with the back of my hand.

The moment he walked in, another man appeared at the doorway. It was the sumo wrestler, and he was dressed in another finely tailored suit. "I filled out your grandmother's questionnaire," he told me, waving a packet of papers.

I figured that he must have been a difficult match if my grandmother made him fill out a questionnaire. Normally, she went by instinct and at most, jotted down notes on notecards.

"Come on in," I said, and stepped behind Bruce Coyle. As I began to shut the door, the mayor drove up the driveway and parked. I turned toward my two matches. "I'll meet you in the kitchen in a minute," I told them. "Help yourself to the Danish on the table."

The mayor stepped out of his car, and another man stepped out of the passenger side. He was an average-sized man with a receding hairline, and a trim mustache. He was wearing a gray suit, and he carried a briefcase.

"Gladie," the mayor yelled, waving. "It's me, and boy, do I have a surprise!"

He walked into the house, and the other man nodded to me. "I'm Gregory Jones," he said.

"Don't tell her, yet," the mayor said. "I want it to be a surprise."

He followed the mayor inside, and I finally shut the door. "Townspeople, I have wondrous news!" he announced.

"We're busy. What is it?" Josephine grumbled.

The mayor chuckled. "Oh, Josephine. You're such a side-slapper! All right, everyone gather around. Move the chairs so you're all looking at me. Boy, oh boy, do I have a surprise. We should have balloons," he said, looking around, as if balloons were going to appear in the parlor. "Oh, well, I guess this will have to do. How are we doing today? Lovely morning, we're having. Don't you love the fresh spring air?"

"Get on with it," Griffin growled. "We have five hundred thousand eggs to deal with."

"Hear that, Mr. Jones?" the mayor said to the man with the briefcase. "We're going all the way with this thing. It's the most exciting world record since Evil Knievel jumped the Grand Canyon."

"What a moron," Alice grumbled. "Evil Knievel never jumped the Grand Canyon."

"Who's Evil Knievel?" a man asked.

The mayor chuckled, again. "We should have a drumroll. Gladie, could you do a drumroll?"

Everyone looked at me. “I don’t have drums,” I said.

“You don’t need drums,” a man shouted at me. “You pretend. Haven’t you ever done a drumroll before? Are you one of those millennials? They don’t know anything.”

“They all got an award at Little League, just for showing up,” another man agreed.

“You know what I got for showing up at Little League?” another man asked. “Nothing.”

“And my mother washed my mouth out with soap if I talked back,” Alice chimed in. “Millennials don’t even know what bar soap is, and they sure haven’t ever had it in their mouths.”

“But they should!” another woman shouted.

“If it’s not in a video game, they don’t know what it is,” Josephine said.

“Pretend it’s a video game,” the mayor told me. “Do a video game drumroll.”

I didn’t play video games, and I had never been in Little League or had gotten a show-up award or any kind of award. But I didn’t think they would believe me, and I didn’t think they would be satisfied until I did a drumroll. Besides, I needed to hear the big news quickly because I had two matches waiting for me in the kitchen.

I slapped my hands against the wall, getting faster. It was

my first drumroll, and it wasn't bad. "Ladies and gentlemen," the mayor began. "Let me introduce you to Gregory Jones from the Paramount World Record office!"

I stopped my drumroll. "What the hell kind of cockamamie world record is that?" Griffin demanded. "What happened to Guinness?"

"This is better than Guinness."

Gregory Jones cleared his throat. "Paramount is a much better deal for Cannes. Let me explain."

That was my cue to duck out. I tip-toed to the kitchen. My matches were in deep conversation, while they scarfed down Danish. They were hitting it off. If only they were gay, I could have killed two birds right there and then.

Speaking of birds, Meryl's parrot flew into the kitchen, landed on a chair, and said something that no one could understand.

"What language is that?" the sumo wrestler asked.

"No idea."

"No clue," Bruce said.

"Maybe Slavic. I have a grandmother from Hungary," the sumo wrestler said.

"I don't know much about birds," I said, eyeing the bird and not making any sudden movements. "Do they bite? Do they have teeth?"

"They have teeth, but only about four or five," Bruce said.

The parrot talked at me again. "No, that's not Hungarian," the sumo wrestler said. "Maybe it's Hindi?"

"Both H languages. That makes sense," I said.

"I've had a terrible time dating," Bruce complained, changing the subject. "I need professional help. Women just don't get me."

Bruce's confession sparked a tidal wave of heartfelt confessions of their needs and desires with love. They didn't want anything out of the ordinary, and my heart went out to them for coming to a point in their lives where they wanted love more than they wanted anything else. It was a turning point in their lives, and they had come to my grandmother for help, and now I was going to help them.

Wait a second. What did Josephine mean by saying she found a murdered body? How did she know it was murdered? Why didn't she tell anyone about it? And why was she telling me now?

"She doesn't have to be a model," the sumo wrestler was telling me. "I just want a girl who understands my passion for sumo and who knows how to cook."

"She does have to be a model for me. I mean she has to at least look like a model," Bruce insisted. "A beautiful, gorgeous woman. Perfect, thin body with a beautiful face and thick, flowing hair. Oh, and she needs to like cats. I have six cats. I love cats. If she doesn't like cats, that's a deal-breaker, even if she's Gisele. You know what I mean?"

Cats. Cooking. No fat. Sumo. I got it. Sure, there was a touch of magic in falling in love, but the bare facts, dirty details went a long way. Finding a model for Bruce would take some doing, but I was getting a good vibe about finding a sumo wrestler fan.

The parrot squawked something unintelligible, and the men looked behind me. I turned around. A blond woman in a tall, bouffant hairdo and four pounds of makeup smiled and pointed her long fingernail at me. "You must be Gladie Burger," she said in a thick New Jersey accent. "I'm Liz Essex. I own Buckstars."

"Nice to meet you," I said. "I met your…"

"Husband? Ford? Yes, that's him. Anyway, I heard that this is the hub of happenings in Cannes. So, I said: 'Liz? If you were a smart woman, you would go to that hub of happenings and hand out coupons to our new and fabulous establishment.' So, here I am," she announced, holding up a handful of coupons. "Do you like coffee? Hot chocolate?" she asked my matches, handing them coupons for a free hot beverage. "We're having a big grand opening party tomorrow. Everyone's welcome!"

She pranced into the other room, and we followed her out. In the parlor, the egg meeting was still going on. The three groups were wrapping up their strategy session on how to manage hundreds of thousands of eggs. The mayor was giddy with joy at the town trying for a celebrity and even happier about his coupon for a free hot beverage on Buckstars grand opening the next day.

"Hate coffee, but love new business," the mayor said. "Coffee gives me the runs. How about you, Mr. Jones? Does coffee give you the runs?"

The representative from the Paramount World Records organization took a step back and his eyes bugged out. It was a typical reaction to our mayor.

"Tea doesn't give me the runs, but I don't like tea," the mayor continued, not waiting for an answer from Mr. Jones. "Then there's soda. That doesn't give me the runs, either, but soda is supposed to give a man diabetes. Or is it shrunken balls? Yes, I think that's it. Shrunken balls. Anyway, time to show you the Historic District to give you an idea of where the action is."

The poor man didn't seem to want to see where the action was. In fact, he seemed like he wanted to flee, and I didn't blame him. But I guessed that a job was a job, and so when the mayor went to leave, Mr. Jones followed him. When he opened the door, Bridget was there. She caught my eye, and I was immediately struck with panic.

She was pale, like she had been punched in the gut and couldn't catch her breath. Something terrible had happened to Bridget. I was struck with a strong fight or flight response, but it turned inside me into a protective, mama bear response.

"Everyone out!" I ordered. "I need to clear the house! Important business!"

There were a few complaints, but the tone of my voice was pretty definite. They grabbed their notebooks, which were full of their plans of attack and Buckstars coupons and shuffled out of the house. I closed the door and hugged Bridget to me.

"Bridget, what's wrong? Do you need a doctor?"

"He's here," she whispered in my ear, her voice gravelly, unnatural, and full of fear. "The baby's father. He's here."

CHAPTER 7

Communication. Without it, a couple is just two people. I don't mean schmaltzy kind of communication and poetry. A man doesn't have to quote Yates. A woman doesn't have to write cards. But they have to communicate. If your matches don't know how, teach them small talk. "Nice hat." "Do you watch Netflix?" Stuff like that. With practice, the small talk turns big. It's the big talk that keeps a relationship alive.

Lesson 83, Matchmaking advice from your
Grandma Zelda

I sat Bridget in the sunroom next to the kitchen, and I brought her a glass of water with a tablespoon of sugar in it, just like my grandmother had taught me to do. I held her hand, and slowly the color returned to her face.

"What happened?" I asked her, gently.

"Gladie, I'm in so much trouble. He's a mean, mean man."

"Did he hurt you? Are you okay?"

"Do you have any liquor?"

"Bridget, you're pregnant. Think of Delano."

She pushed her glasses up her nose and squinted at me, like she was trying to gauge just where to punch me in the face. "How about tequila? I heard that tequila is fine for pregnant women."

"Really? Okay, I can get you some tequila." I didn't know anything about pregnant women. The whole thing made me feel icky. I mean, how did the poor baby breathe in there? And wasn't it smooshed between her poop canal and her pee pee area?

I didn't know anything about anatomy, either.

"No!" Bridget yelled, grabbing me and giving me a good shake. "Don't let me drink tequila! What's wrong with you? Do you want me to brain damage my baby?"

"No! I mean, only if you want to." I wiped sweat off my face. Pregnant women were a minefield. I never knew what to say except for agreeing with them.

"Gladie, I don't want to brain damage my baby."

"Okay. Noted."

"Not that I'm judging women with substance abuse problems," she said, earnestly. "It's not their fault. They're gripped by the power of mood-enhancing and mood-altering drugs. It's not their fault, Gladie."

I nodded. "Uh huh. I think we might have gotten off track."

She blinked. "Oh, right. Bradford Blythe."

"Is that his name? Delano's father?"

"Remember that bookkeeping conference I went to? Well, there was another conference at the hotel, too. An evil one-percenter conference of...of...of..."

"Of what?" I breathed. "Sex trafficking? Torturers? IRS?"

Bridget took a deep breath, as if she was gathering strength to tell me how much she weighed. "Venture capitalists," she squeaked. "And there was a bar, and he was tall, and he had an expense account. The evils of the sour apple-tini, Gladie. They're so good going down."

She was right. I had never drunk a sour apple-tini, but I had danced on barrels naked once after three Long Island iced teas. I so related.

"Most of it's a blur," she said, running her fingers through her curly hair, making it stand up on end. "I remember that he was a terrible kisser, but he could take my bra off with two fingers. And then there was the thing about his penis."

I bit my lower lip. I didn't know if I should ask her about his penis or wait for her to give me the skinny. She wasn't meeting my eyes. She was looking everywhere but at me. I pretended I didn't care about her baby daddy's penis. *Think about puppies. Think about dirty dishes. Think about…her baby daddy's penis.* Nope, it was impossible to pretend I didn't care.

"What? What about his penis?" I asked. "Was it freaky? Was it not human?"

"What do you mean not human? Like a dog?"

"No, I mean robotic or something. Bionic. We can rebuild him, make his penis stronger than he was before. Like that."

"No, not like that. Like he said his penis was very clean and he had had a vasectomy, so we didn't need protection. No condoms."

Bridget leaned forward. This time her eyes were on mine, her face less than an inch away from me. Her breath smelled like Oreos and asparagus. "Gladie," she said, her voice deadly serious. "I trusted a man…when he was naked."

She had fallen into the classic trap. Naked man propaganda. If I had had a nickel for every time a woman had fallen for it, I would have had a crap ton of nickels.

"So you got pregnant," I guessed.

"And I got a case of chlamydia. Bastard with his penis."

"Wow."

"And it's not like he ever told me his name. All I got was Brad. Brad. My son's father's name is Brad. Can you imagine? Me and a Brad? But I didn't look for him. A guy from the conference saw me pregnant and reported it back to his buddy. Damned patriarchal, misogynistic, buddy system."

It was rotten luck.

"And then the threats started. He doesn't even want Delano. He just doesn't want me to have him. He's part of some big family, and he doesn't want a son wandering around out there to embarrass him."

She told me about an increasing level of harassment. He had hired a private investigator to stalk her and find out everything about her. She had offered to give him fifty percent custody when he threatened to burn down her house, but he wanted full custody.

"Why didn't you come to me? To Spencer? He could have helped," I said.

"You don't know who this guy is. When I say one-percent, I mean one-percent. Power, Gladie. He's connected."

"And now he's here?"

Tears streamed down her face. "He's here to ruin my life. Ruin my baby's life," she said, touching her belly.

There are times in a person's life when all fear disappears, and it's replaced with a titanic determination. Better than any drug. It was best friend superhero superpowers. Nothing could stop me. I was going to protect Bridget and little Delano with my last breath.

I was pissed off.

There was a soft knock on the window of Bridget's Volkswagen Bug. She unlocked the door, and Lucy slipped into the back seat behind Bridget. Lucy was dressed in tight black yoga pants, a black, long-sleeved angora sweater, a silk scarf on her head, and black stiletto heels.

"I'm here, girlfriends. Where is that no account, mouth-breathing, low-life, belly of a snake, lying penis man? I brought night vision goggles for everyone," Lucy added, holding up three pairs of goggles.

"Maybe we shouldn't do this," Bridget said. "It's an invasion of privacy. It's like we're the Patriot Act or something. And you know, I protested the Patriot Act."

"I remember," Lucy said. "You climbed on top of Chik'n Lik'n with that sign."

"We're just doing reconnaissance," I said, taking one of the goggles. "How does this work?"

"Flip the switch. It's like magic," Lucy said. I did, and all of a sudden I could see through the night. We were in front of Bar

None, and there were people coming and going down the alley next door. They were carrying egg crates, which I assumed were filled with eggs. I still hadn't boiled an egg.

"Look at that," Lucy said. "I think that's a black-market egg thing happening. The truck from Sacramento was delayed, you know. Something about a flat tire. Or was it Aliens?"

"Aliens?" I asked.

"There's been a lot of alien sightings, lately," Bridget explained. "Sean the plumber said aliens removed his frontal lobe during a commercial break when he was watching the fights on television."

"That's rough," I said. I didn't know what a frontal lobe was, but it sounded important.

Lucy grunted. "I can't wait for the egg hunt to be over. The whole town stinks of eggs. I'm ruined for eggs Benedict for the rest of my life. Anyway, I'm buying the baskets for the little ones. Twenty thousand of them. I don't know who's in charge of luring twenty thousand children here, though."

A man walked up to Bar None and opened the door. "That's him," Bridget gasped. "What are we doing? We can't do this. My baby. My baby. I'll just run away to Siberia."

"I don't think labor rights are very progressive in Siberia, darlin'," Lucy pointed out.

"I don't know what to do," she cried.

"I do. Stay here," I said. Handing my goggles to Lucy, I opened the door and got out.

Bar None was blaring Fleetwood Mac, and I could hear it before I walked in. I opened the door. Inside, it was practically empty with most of the town elsewhere, busy boiling eggs. But Bradford Blythe, otherwise known as Brad with the clean, spermless penis, was there, sitting at a table with Spencer's contractor, Urijah.

I sat at a nearby stool at the bar and tried to eavesdrop. "What can I get you?" the bartender asked me.

"Peanuts."

"Huh?"

"Shh!"

Bradford and Urijah were in a heated conversation. Bradford was angry and Urijah was scared. But I couldn't make out the words because Stevie Nicks was singing too loudly. I scooted the stool a little, but it would have been suspicious if I had scooted it clear over to their table.

"Here's your peanuts," the bartender said. "Usually people come in to drink."

I grabbed the bowl from him and put a handful of nuts in my mouth. "Thanks." Bridget's baby's daddy stood and walked toward the bathroom. I trotted to the table. "What are you doing with him?" I asked Urijah.

"Huh?"

"Him. Him. What are you doing with him? Are you plotting something horrible? Because if you are, I'm going to make sure you eat through a straw for the rest of your life."

His face drained of color, and he looked around, as if he was expecting me to have backup. I did have backup, but they were in a Volkswagen Bug outside. "How did you know?"

"I know everything," I growled. I had him where I wanted him. He had nowhere to escape. I was going to squeeze the information out of him.

"I'm outta here," he said and bolted for the door. In five seconds, he was gone.

"That didn't go right," I said to the empty table. "That was the opposite of going right."

I looked over at the bathroom sign. It was now or never.

I got to the door just as Brad was leaving. He was very tall and good-looking, and I hated him instantly. He gave me a wolfish grin and put his hand on the wall above my head. "Hey, babe," he said.

My skin crawled. "You need to leave town," I said.

"Not before you and I get to know each other," he purred, gliding his finger along my chin line. I slapped his hand away.

"You're going to leave town and never try to contact

Bridget again."

He put his hands in his pockets and rocked on his heels. "Oh. I see. That's why you're here. Well, you can tell that bitch that I've just gotten started. And this little thing you're doing here is going on my list of complaints. You better hope I don't get a bruise or bump leaving here, or you're going to wind up in jail."

I swallowed. He was serious. He arched an eyebrow and grinned, again.

"Women like you disappear every day, and they're never found. And you know why? Because nobody cares. Women are an easy commodity. Like eggs. Who cares about a few broken eggs? Nobody."

Ironic he was talking about eggs because with six days until the Easter egg hunt, a few broken eggs would have triggered a psychotic break in all kinds of people in town. But he wasn't talking about eggs. He was talking about me and other women, and I wondered how many women had been a victim to his bullying. And worse.

I pushed down my fear because I had to be brave for Bridget. "You leave her alone," I squeaked. "You know, we have an alien problems here. You wouldn't want your frontal lobe to go missing."

"Huh?"

"You heard me."

I didn't know what I was saying, and he obviously didn't, either. In any case, I had made no progress at all. I would have pleaded, begged, and negotiated with him, but I was certain none of that would have helped. Bradford Blythe was a bully, and bullies only responded to being bullied. I was going to have to call in bigger guns. Big, giant guns.

Spencer guns.

Back in Bridget's car, I sort of told Lucy and Bridget what happened, leaving out the scary threats. "We're at an impasse," I said, diplomatically. "But all is not lost. I'm going to have Spencer run him out of town."

Lucy didn't look convinced. She had a point. Spencer wasn't much for running men out of town. He stupidly was a fan of law and order. But Lucy's husband, Harry, was the run-a-man-out-of-town type. He would do it, if Lucy asked him. I gnawed on the inside of my cheek, thinking about it. I was more or less a fan of law and order, too. This was a domestic situation that had gotten way out of hand, but I didn't know if it could be resolved, considering who and what Bradford Blythe was.

Bridget started her car. "I wish I had never gone to that conference. I wish he were dead. My life would be so much easier if he was just dead. Dead, dead, dead."

In my experience, dead didn't make anything easier. In fact, it usually complicated matters. But I didn't tell Bridget that. She was overwhelmed and despondent and for the moment, she was fantasizing about making her problems disappear as easily as a stopped heart.

Lucy got in her car, and Bridget drove me home through town. "I promise we'll get this worked out," I told her, but she didn't respond. "Oh my God, look at that."

As we passed Buckstars, I saw Ruth Fletcher climbing onto the Buckstars sign.

"What's she doing?" Bridget asked.

"Her worst. She's doing her worst. Never get on Ruth's bad side."

By the time I got home, Spencer was asleep upstairs. I checked on my grandmother to see if she needed something, and she was up watching an infomercial on TV and needlepointing. I sat on the bed.

"I've never seen you needlepoint, Grandma."

"Dumbest activity every invented. Bird's pedicurist brought it with a tuna casserole. The casserole was delicious so I'm suffering through this stupid handicraft in order not to hurt her feelings." She put the needlepoint down and studied me. "Uh oh. You're suffering, too. It's hard when our friends are in pain, and we can't help them."

"I can't help her?"

"I'm foggy about Bridget, dolly. I'm seeing coffee and tears. That's it."

My heart raced. Bridget was one of the kindest people I had ever met, and she was my best friend. I didn't want to see her hurt. I took a quick shower to wash away the evil Bradford Blythe from me and slipped into bed next to Spencer. I laid on my side, nestled my head in the crook of his arm and put my hand on his six-pack, washboard abs.

"Are you sleeping?" I asked, and Spencer answered with a snore. "Are you awake? Are you? Are you?" I gave him a little shove. He turned on his side and pulled me in close to him, like spoons. "Are you still on vacation? Are you going back to work soon?"

"I wish I wasn't, but I'm going back in the morning," he said, his voice low and thick with sleep. "The eggs thing is bad enough, but now aliens are accosting townspeople left and right. Crazy-ass town. I'm a real law enforcement officer, Pinky. I don't do aliens."

"I think Bridget needs your help."

"I told her I'm not going to be a surrogate male figure in the delivery room. I'm not going to sit at the mouth of her vagina to imbue her son with male energy. Nope. Nope. No matter what you say, I'm not going to do it."

"No, I mean she needs your help as a law enforcement officer. As police chief. As a macho, alpha male who loves me."

"Uh oh. What have you been up to?" Spencer asked. "Not

the murdered girl in the bed, again."

"No. This is about Bridget. She's got trouble." I told him about the baby daddy, or at least part of it. I didn't tell Spencer about my conversation with him or about the night goggles. But I made it clear that Bridget was scared of him and that he was fighting for custody.

"Sounds like she needs a good lawyer."

"Right now she's just scared and needs some breathing room. Can you give her some breathing room and talk to him?"

Spencer turned me so that I was lying on my back and he moved on top of me, supporting his weight with his forearms on the bed on either side of my head. "I'll talk to him in the morning. Will that do? I'm going back to work tomorrow. I mean, today. It's past midnight. You know what that means?"

"I turn into a pumpkin?"

"It's your birthday. You're a year older."

"That doesn't sound like a good thing," I said. The only light in the room was coming from the clock, but it was just enough to make out his outline and know that he was drinking me in with his eyes. He was giving off heat and enough testosterone to make a bull blush. I reached up and touched his face, and as my fingers reached his lips, he kissed them softly. Sensually.

"It's a good thing. It means you're the birthday girl. It means you get what you want for the whole day. That's why I want to take you out, to give you what you want."

"What about now? Will you give me what I want now?"

"What do you want?" he asked, his voice seductive.

"A million dollars and a Snickers bar."

"Hey, baby, I've got your Snickers bar right here."

"And the million dollars?"

"How about something that's *worth* a million dollars?"

"You think very highly about yourself."

"At least let me give you your first birthday present now."

"It sounds more like a birthday present for you. Not me."

"Oh, Pinky, you wound me. Don't you trust me to be…generous?"

"Okay. I'll let you be generous. Happy birthday to me."

CHAPTER 8

Happy! You have the gift, dolly. So, you will have many happy times in your matchmaking career, making happy matches. But I have to warn you. Matchmaking is a pain in the tuches because of the hiccoughs. Lots and lots of hiccoughs. You know the ones...when everything is going right and then all of a sudden it isn't. But it's just a hiccough. Hold your breath and get through it.

Lesson 84, Matchmaking advice from your Grandma Zelda

Spencer's birthday present had turned me into a giggling fool. I couldn't stop giggling. Even though I was worried about Bridget, angry at Bradford Blythe, irritated by Terri, overwhelmed by the Easter egg hunt committee, and clueless about my two matches, everything made me happy. No, it wasn't about my birthday. It was about being in love, which also made me overwhelmed and clueless and even worried. But love was a funny thing. It made a person happy no matter how scared and miserable they were.

And I was singing a lot, too. I sang in the shower. I sang getting dressed. Orgasms were great for singing.

Spencer was up and smiling, too. He was dressed for work in his tailored black suit, his face covered in just enough stubble, and his hair thick and wavy with an imperceptible amount of product in it. He was hot, hot, hot. I would have jumped him right there and then, if I wasn't already saddlesore.

He shot me a Prince-Charming-master-of-the-universe look, and I shot him a Sleeping-Beauty-in-the-castle look back. "I'm taking you out this evening," he said. "Get ready."

"You mean buff and polish?"

He arched an eyebrow and smirked his little smirk. "I mean emotionally and psychologically."

"Uh oh."

"Exactly. All right, here I go. I wish Remington wasn't away at a conference. I'm the only one on the force with half of a brain."

My heart pounded in my chest. Today Spencer would probably find out about my involvement in Terri's biting and couch traffic accident. There was a fifty-fifty chance that he wouldn't want to celebrate my birthday by the end of the day.

Oh, well. I was still happy and singing.

Spencer left for work, and I checked on my grandmother. Her friends were already there, and they were eating breakfast, so I decided to treat myself to a latte at Tea Time.

It was a gorgeous spring morning. The air was sweet, there was no humidity, and a soft breeze was blowing. A couple of speedwalkers waved at me as they passed, and there was only a slight smell of eggs in the air. It was like all of the problems that I had only the night before had vanished. What a perfect day for a birthday. I felt like anything was possible.

It looked like Tea Time was bursting at the seams with a large crowd outside, but when I got up closer, I realized the crowd was there for the Grand Opening of Buckstars, each person clutching a coupon in their hand. The Buckstars sign had been vandalized, and it now read *Corporate Shill Fuckstars* in bright red paint.

Retail was brutal.

I opened the door to Tea Time and walked in. There wasn't a soul in the place except for Ruth and her grand-niece Julie, who was sweeping up a broken plate.

"The fascist, corporate coffee is next door!" Ruth bellowed when I walked in.

"It's me, Ruth!" I bellowed back.

"If I see a coupon in your hand, you'll never be allowed in

this establishment again. You hear me?"

"I hear you," I said, putting my hands on the bar counter. "The usual, please, Ruth. I need your coffee."

She nodded, as if she had been deciding whether I was a good guy or a bad guy and came out on the side of good guy. "Okay."

"And it's my birthday, but you don't have to do anything special. Maybe a little cake or a tasteful gift, but nothing big."

"Ha. Ha. Very funny," she said, turning on the espresso machine.

"Just kidding. I didn't think you would give me something for my birthday."

She heated the milk. "Maybe I should get you what you've gotten me for my past eighty birthdays. Would you like that?"

She meant nothing. I had never gotten her anything. I was terrible with presents, mainly because I was poor and had no talents for crafts.

"Stop singing," she ordered.

"Was I singing?"

"Yes. Some Enchanted Evening. You don't have the voice for that song, Gladie."

Ruth finished preparing my latte and put it in front of me

on the bar. Then, she put a plate down next to it. It was a chocolate chip scone with a candle in the middle. She flicked a lighter and lit the candle, shocking the hell out of me.

"Don't say anything," she said. "Just blow the damned thing out."

"I can't say thank you?"

"No."

"Not even a grunt of gratitude?"

"The wax is melting onto the scone that I made with my arthritic hands. So, if you don't blow the damned thing out, I'm going to have to throw away the scone, and it might be the last one I ever make because I'm older than dirt and could die any second. But sure, you take your time since you're going to live forever. I get it. The arrogance of youth. What is a scone to you? Nothing. What's my hard work to you? Nothing. You're the instant gratification generation. You don't work for anything. You want it now and you get it now. Fingers on your phone all the time. Smartphones! What an oxymoron. They should be called dumbphones because they make folks dumb. Click. Click. Click. Nobody talks to anybody anymore. They just click their phones. Facebook, Twitter, YouPube."

"YouTube."

"Whatever. You should be ashamed of yourself that you know that. It used to be we wanted to know things. Real things. Now you think you're a genius because you know YouTube. What a stupid name! Damned smartphone, corporate coffee morons."

"I have a flip phone, Ruth. I found it on the street."

"You know what I mean."

She took a breath. Her face was red, and I hoped she wasn't going to have a stroke because that would have made my birthday a real downer.

"May I blow out my candle now?" I asked.

"Are you baiting me, girl?"

I blew, and the flame went out. Ruth slapped a small, wrapped gift onto the bar. "Here. Happy birthday."

I swear that real tears filled my eyes. Ruth had already given me her car and free lattes for a year, and now she had remembered my birthday. I didn't know why she was being so nice to me, since she was the orneriest woman on the planet.

"Thank you, Ruth," I said, opening the box. Inside, there was a beautiful silk scarf. Blue and green with an intricate design. I had never had something so beautiful.

"It's not new, mind you," she growled. "I picked it up in France right before the war. That's World War Two to you."

"France? Really?"

"I thought the colors would bring out your eyes. Let me show you how to tie it around your neck."

She walked around the bar and tied it for me.

"There. Just like I thought," she said, not looking me in the eyes.

"You look pretty," Julie squeaked at me, the dustbin in her hand. "Like an old-timey movie star, like Julia Roberts."

"Thank you so much, Ruth," I told her. Under normal circumstances, I would have given her a hug and a kiss on the cheek, but I thought that would make her angry at me, and Ruth was terrifying when she was pissed off.

"Drink your latte before it gets cold, or don't you care about coffee, either?"

She made a show of wiping down the clean bar, and I made a show of sipping the latte and nibbling the scone.

Julie dumped the broken plate in the trash and walked up to me. "Gladie," she squeaked. "I'm so scared."

"Did you set fire to your bed, again?"

"No, not for a month. I'm worried about... about... about... Fred."

She wiped her nose on her sleeve. Fred was her boyfriend, and my first match. He was Spencer's desk sergeant, and when Spencer said there wasn't a person with half a brain on the force, Fred was included in that statement.

"More butt smuggling?" I asked. When Terri arrived in

town as the new hotshot detective, she put Fred on butt searching detail. It was surprising how many criminals hid things in their butts. Poor Fred had had a nervous breakdown because of the butt thing, but Terri had been demoted, and I had figured that Fred's butt searching duties were over, but maybe I was wrong.

"No, it's worse than butts. It's that woman. The pretty one. The one who looks like a supermodel."

"Terri Williams." My nemesis. The woman who hated me and kept giving me tickets for being annoying. No matter what I did, I couldn't get her to like me, and she wasn't a good woman to have not like a person.

"She's after my Fred," Julie blubbered, her nose running down into her mouth. "She wants to take him away from me."

I blinked. "Wait a second. Terri is after Fred? What do you mean? Like she's trying to kill him?"

"No. That wouldn't be so bad," Ruth said, interrupting. "That hot number is after our doofus Fred to snag him. Get him in her bed forever. Bed him and wed him. She's mighty determined."

It was crazy. It was ludicrous. It was gravity that made things fly. It was left going right and right going wrong. Terri had told me that she was after a man in the police department, but it had to be Spencer. That made more sense. And that's why she hated me. She loved Spencer and Spencer loved me. So, she hated me. Right? She wanted me out of the way so she could get Spencer. Right?

"If she loves Fred, why does she hate me?" I asked Julie and Ruth.

"Maybe she knows you," Ruth said.

"I've been so nice to her," I complained. I was a nice person, and I wasn't used to people hating me for no reason. It made me crazy.

"I heard you bit her," Julie squeaked.

"Merry Ferry bit her. I was just there."

"I heard you pushed her in front of a motorized couch," Ruth said.

That was sort of true. "I'm a nice person," I insisted. My birthday joy was flying out of my head.

"Can you help me?" Julie asked. "Fred and I were going to get married this summer. We were thinking July fourth so there could be fireworks."

"Fireworks?" Ruth asked. "You two? You'll blow up the town."

Julie and Fred were getting married? My first match was going to get married in July. I was a success. Suddenly, I was filled with professional pride and purpose. I had made a real match.

But Terri wanted to derail that. I had to stop her, but short of killing her, I didn't know how.

Then my brain clicked into place.

"What did you say?" I asked Julie.

"I didn't say anything."

"Yes you did. Before. You said Terri was the pretty one. The one who looked like what?"

"A supermodel. Actually, she looks like Gisele."

I smiled, and I felt a weight lift off of me. The solution was crystal clear.

I took Julie's hand in mine. "I'll help you," I promised.

After I finished my coffee, I walked out, and Ruth went outside with me. Buckstars was still doing bang-up business. Ruth stared at it with a scowl plastered on her face, and she stood with her arms crossed in front of her. "I like your sign," I told Ruth.

"It's just the beginning."

"You're not going to set fire to it, are you?"

"Don't be silly. A fire could take down Tea Time. A flood, on the other hand, would be effective."

I watched as half of the town went in with their coupons and came out with a free hot beverage. Then, I saw him. Bradford Blythe, Bridget's baby daddy and her tormentor. He looked around and walked into Buckstars. My stress returned, and any urge to sing vanished.

"See ya later, Ruth," I said. "Thanks for my birthday presents."

I quick-stepped into Buckstars. I didn't have a plan. It was stupid to confront him again. Spencer had already promised to handle him, and I had only managed to make the bastard more aggressive when I had spoken to him. No, it was stupid to follow him into Buckstars. But I couldn't stop myself. It was like evil was a magnet that I was helpless to resist.

The small coffee place had more people than Studio 54 on Saturday night in 1977. Brad walked through the crowd, looking around as if he was searching for someone in particular. In front of me, Ford Essex, the owner of the shop was watching Bradford, too. He watched his every movement. And he was scared. Did they know each other, or was Ford a good judge of character?

A hand gripped my shoulder. "Gladie, there you are." I turned around to see Josephine. Her hair was a large frizzball around her head, and she was holding a coffee to-go cup. "Look at me. No, I haven't stuck my finger in an outlet. I boiled eggs all night long. I'm not the only one. Look around."

I looked around. Brad had disappeared into the crowd. Josephine was right, though. There were at least a dozen frizzballs in the room. The town was boiling eggs nonstop. The caffeine break must have been welcome for them.

"We're never going to make it," Josephine continued. "There's too much to do, and we're a tiny town, you know. Not enough cooks in our kitchen. Our stupid, illustrious leader has really socked us one this time. Look at him over there with his world records guy. He's been showing him off all around town, like he's George Clooney or Barack Obama. Do you believe they were at my house at eleven last night to make sure I was boiling the eggs correctly?"

The mayor and Gregory Jones were enjoying their free drinks. Jones looked tired. His tie was askew, and one of his buttons was unbuttoned. I wondered how a man chose a career in world records. It was one of the few jobs I never had.

The mayor caught my eye and walked over to me. "Hello, Gladie. Isn't it fabulous?"

"Fabulous."

"Look at this Buckstars. We're becoming very cosmopolitan, don't you think?" He didn't wait for me to answer. "Look at these to-go cups with logos on them. Just like the big city. Next we'll get a movie theater or a Tesla dealership. The sky's the limit! Oh, there's Pierre. I need to make sure he's pulling his egg weight. Hidey-ho, Pierre!"

He cornered a small man with glasses, who looked horrified to be cornered.

"Seems like it's going well," Liz Essex said, grabbing me when the mayor left. "I knew a coffee place would do well. So much better than the ceramic cat store that was here before."

"I guess ceramic cats don't do the business they once did," I said, scanning the shop for Brad. I couldn't find him.

"It might be the dead body buried here that turned customers off," she said.

My head snapped back to give my full attention to the Starbucks owner. "What did you say? A dead body's buried here?"

"You didn't know? That's the rumor, anyway. Crazy cat lady buried a body under the floor we're standing on." I looked down at my feet. The floor had been retiled in a non-threatening beige.

"You found a body?"

"No. Between you and me, I think everyone assumes that the remodel would have uncovered it, but we didn't do any actual digging. It could literally be right under our feet as we're standing here." She giggled and put her hand over her mouth. "Oops. Maybe I shouldn't have told you that. Let's keep this between us." She waved at her husband and said something to him in a foreign language that I couldn't make out.

She walked into the crowd without saying another word to me. I was in the middle of the crush with people swirling around me. I needed to take a step back, closer to the wall to make heads or tails out of the crowd and try to find Brad. I began to push my way to the wall when I picked up a voice, which was just a little louder than a whisper.

"Sometimes murder is deserved. The wild need to be tamed, and when they can't be tamed, they need to be extinguished."

I spun around, searching for the person who was speaking, but I couldn't figure out who had said it. It was Grand Central in the coffee place. It was amazing how the prospect of getting a cup of coffee for free instead of the regular four-dollars brought people in. I searched the faces, trying to determine which face would voice the virtues of murder.

And that's when I finally saw him. Bradford Blythe was walking with a purpose toward the back of Buckstars. I was wedged near the sugar station, unable to follow him. "Excuse me. Excuse me," I repeated over and over, but I couldn't make any progress. I searched for him again, but he had vanished into the back of the store. But I saw someone else who I wasn't expecting.

Bridget was there.

"Oh my God," I breathed, when I spotted her. She was heading in the same direction where Brad had disappeared.

My heart stopped, and I was having a hard time breathing. "Bridget," I gasped. "Don't do anything stupid." I watched as she vanished into the back, too. I was imbued with a renewed sense of purpose. If I didn't know why I was following Brad, I was certain that I had to be there for Bridget. No good could come from her meeting him alone.

"Excuse me. Excuse me," I said, trying to push my way through the coffee drinkers. I was making progress at a snail's pace. I was worried about my friend. What would her baby's father say to her? What would he do to her? He had threatened me, and he didn't even know me. I couldn't imagine the lengths he would go to hurt Bridget. "Coffee emergency!" I shouted, pulling out the big guns. "And I smoked a cigarette, too! You know what that means!"

They knew what that meant. They parted like the Red Sea, allowing me a straight shot to the bathrooms at the back of the shop. I went into the women's bathroom, but Bridget wasn't there. Ditto the men's bathroom. Another door said "Staff Only," and I opened that door.

Finally, I found Bridget. She was crouched over Brad with a bloody knife in her hand. And Brad was lying prostrate, in a pool of blood.

And he was dead, dead, dead.

CHAPTER 9

Matchmaking emergencies are weird, meshugana ones, dolly. Most of them fall into three categories: Before dates, During dates, After dates. Lots of anguish about dates. I've shaved more than one woman's legs before a date. I've had to save a woman trapped on a Ferris Wheel during a date. And I've taken quite a few men for VD checks after their dates. Emergencies at the time seem huge, but later—like right now—they seem ridiculous and easy. So, when you're faced with an emergency, know that it'll be all right. Like they say, in a hundred years, who'll care? Of course, in a hundred years, we'll be dead.

Lesson 96, Matchmaking advice from your Grandma Zelda

"Wha… huh… uh…" I stammered. I took in the scene in jagged images. Multiple knife wounds. Brad's bloody face. His open mouth. His open eyes. Bridget's hand, holding the knife and shaking. Her eyes, unblinking. Her skin, drained of color.

"Bridget? Are you okay?"

She didn't answer. She was in shock. What was I supposed to do for shock? I was probably in shock, too. My stomach was protesting, and I forced myself not to faint. Bridget needed me, and that gave me strength. I kneeled down next to her.

"Bridget, drop the knife. Please. Drop the knife and get up. You shouldn't be here. Please, Bridget. I love you, sweetie. Let me help you."

Nothing. She didn't move, didn't flinch, didn't blink.

Then, there was a scream. At first I thought it was me or at the very least Bridget, but as hard as it was to believe, we weren't screaming. A coupon-bearing coffee drinker, who had taken a wrong turn on her way to the toilets had stumbled onto a murdered man, who apparently drowned in his own blood. She was the one screaming.

"Murder! Murder! The bookkeeper did it! She's got a gun!" she screamed while flailing her arms around, like she was the robot on *Lost in Space.*

"She doesn't have a gun! It's a knife!" I yelled at her.

"A gun! A gun! Run for your lives!"

"It's a knife!" I hollered back at her, but she was already gone. She ran out into the crowd, screaming that the bookkeeper had a gun. Getting up, I peeked out the door and watched as panic hit Buckstars. To-go cups flew up in the air, and coffee spilled everywhere.

There was screaming and running. I didn't blame them. I would have done the same thing. There was nothing I could do to calm the situation. It just had to wear itself out. Meanwhile, I went back to Bridget. She hadn't moved a muscle.

I knelt down next to her, again. "Let go of the knife," I told her, softly. She didn't react. "Come on, let me help you."

I heard footsteps in the hall, and then I smelled a familiar cologne. It was Spencer coming to the rescue. "No, Pinky. Don't touch a thing," he said, walking into the tiny room. "Come over here. Let me handle it."

"It's not what it looks like," I told him, but I didn't know if that was true. As far as I knew, it was totally what it looked like. But the Bridget I knew would never take a life, no matter how much of a bad guy he was. She had a total respect for life. She was the queen of empathy.

"I need you to leave the room now, Pinky."

"I'm not leaving her. She's my best friend, and she needs me."

"You want me to Tase her, boss?" It was Terri. She was hovering behind Spencer, and she had a Taser in her hand.

"Get out of here. Take statements outside," he ordered in

his bossiest authoritarian voice.

"But..."

"Do it," he growled, and she listened. When she was gone, he directed his bossy voice to me. "Pinky, if you're not going to leave, back away from Bridget. Stand against the wall."

"Be nice to her," I pleaded.

"Back away from her, now."

I started to cry. It was a quiet kind of crying with lots of tears, snot, and sniffing. But I did what he said and stood with my back to the wall. Spencer put cloth booties over his shiny, leather shoes and disposable gloves on his hands.

He squatted next to Bridget. Her curls had fallen over her face, and he tucked them behind her ear. "You're going to be fine. I promise," he said, softly. His bossy voice was long gone. His dreamy, I'll-take-care-of-you voice had replaced it. I loved that voice.

My tears kept flowing. Spencer gently took Bridget's arm and removed the knife from her hand. She looked at him, as if she was noticing him for the first time. "What are you doing here?" she asked him.

Two paramedics stepped into the doorway. They had a stretcher and a large box of medical supplies. Spencer put a finger up in the air, directing them to stop in their tracks.

"I'm here to make sure you're okay," Spencer told Bridget.

"Oh. I don't feel well."

"I know. We're going to have you checked out at the hospital."

"I'm going with her," I said.

"Yes, we're going to have you checked out, too," Spencer said.

"I'm fine," I said and blubbered, loudly.

"The hospital is in negotiation with the nurse's union. I'm not sure I should go there until they work out the benefits package," Bridget told Spencer.

Spencer helped her up, holding her close, her bloody clothes staining his expensive suit forever. He walked her to the stretcher, and they helped her on to it, all the while, taking her vitals and those of her baby.

I followed them out, but Spencer stopped me. "You all right, Pinky?" he asked, his eyes sparkling with what could have been tears, but I wasn't sure.

"I'm worried about Bridget."

"Okay."

He walked me out, and Bridget, Spencer, and I got in the ambulance together. The mayor was on the sidewalk, talking to the

Buckstars refugees.

"Back to your eggs, townspeople," he bellowed. "Nothing to see here. Get back to your eggs. Remember the eggs!"

The hospital waiting room had orange tiled floor and green walls. That's what I focused on while I waited. They had brought Bridget in immediately when we arrived, in order to check the baby. Spencer had gone with her for police business, but I was told to stay here.

"What're you in for?" a man sitting next to me asked.

"I think I'm in shock or just grossed out. What are you in for? Gallbladder?"

"Aliens."

I scooted a little away from him. "Aliens?"

He pointed to his forehead. There was a drop of dried blood there, like he had popped a pimple. "They tried to cut out my brain. Normally, they suck it out through your ear, you know?"

"Uh…"

"But these aliens they got around here now are coming after us right through the noggin."

"What do the aliens look like?" I asked. I didn't believe in aliens, but I wanted to play on the safe side and know what I should be looking out for.

"Don't know. I was sleeping when they attacked. My dog scared them off. I also have a ghost in my house. He's got horns. A bastard when it rains. Bad weather makes him angry."

I nodded. Finally, the nurse called me back to the emergency room, and I was given a clean bill of health. Then, I was allowed to visit Bridget, who was two beds down and guarded by Terri, while Spencer was on his phone, barking orders.

"Be careful what you say to her," Terri sneered at me. "I'm watching you."

I didn't like that Terri was standing between me and my best friend. I didn't like that Terri had been trying to break up my first match and forcing Fred to look up people's butts. So, I broke. I flipped out on Terri, forgetting that I was supposed to try to make her like me.

"You listen to me, Terri," I spat, punctuating my words by poking her chest with my index finger. "That's my best friend in that bed over there, and she's scared. So, I'm going to help her. And you're not going to get in my way."

"Your friend had a bloody knife in her hand. You should choose your friends more wisely." She took her ticket book out and started writing me another one.

"What's that for?" I asked, trying to look at the ticket.

She clutched the book close to her chest. "Interfering with hospital guarding and being annoying."

"Oh, come on," I said.

"Gladie, come here," Bridget called. I walked inside her room, stuck my tongue out at Terri, and shut the door. Going to Bridget's bedside, I held her hand.

"You shouldn't antagonize her like that," Bridget told me.

"I've been trying to make friends, but she's impossible."

"Well, the antagonizing thing isn't working for you, either."

"You're right," I said. "I have to kill her with kindness. But why are we talking about that now? We have more important things to talk about."

"The baby's fine," Bridget said. She was wearing her hoot owl glasses, but her blue eye shadow had smeared down her face. The blood had been washed off, and the color had returned to her face.

"I'm so glad. What happened with Brad?"

"He called me late last night and said terrible things. He threatened me if I wouldn't meet him this morning. I thought I could talk some reason into him."

"And then what happened?"

"Nothing. I went into the back room, and there he was with a knife in his chest. At first, I didn't understand what was happening. I thought maybe he was playing a terrible joke on me. I grabbed the knife and pulled. Blood spurted out when I took out the knife. Blood everywhere. That's when everything went black."

"You went into shock."

"I went into shock," she agreed.

"Who killed him? Do you have any idea?"

"It could have been anyone."

"Anyone who had ever met him," I agreed.

The door opened, and Spencer walked in. His suit was stained with dried blood.

"Do you have any suspects?" I asked him.

He arched an eyebrow and cocked his head to the side. "Gladie," he said, dragging out my name, like he was chastising a small child.

An uncomfortable silence descended on the room. I looked at Spencer and then to Bridget and back again. "You don't mean," I began.

"Bridget, I'm going to have to read you your rights," Spencer said, gently.

"I know my rights. Why are you going to read them to

me?" Bridget asked.

I stomped my foot. "Spencer Bolton, you're not going to do this."

"Gladie, this is my job. This is what I do. You have to stay out of it."

"What do you do?" Bridget asked. "What do you...Oh," she said, finally understanding. "But I didn't kill him, Spencer. I found him there."

"This is standard procedure, Bridget. You were found at the scene of the crime with the murder weapon in your hand. I'm going to have to arrest you."

I stomped my foot, again. "If you do this, Spencer Bolton, I will never let you be generous with me again!"

The door opened, and Lucy stormed in. She was holding up a thick wad of cash, and she was tugging an old man in an expensive suit behind her. "Don't say a word, Bridget, darlin'," she cried. "Don't say a mother lovin' word. I have your bail money and your lawyer. He could get Manson off, so you have nothing to worry about."

"I'm not Manson," Bridget said.

"Of course you're not, darlin'. Spencer, who do I give this money to?"

Lucy wasn't lying about her lawyer. He got Bridget out on her own recognizance. Of course, it was also a small town, and Bridget was the judge's bookkeeper, and it was two days before taxes were due. And she was pregnant, and nobody wanted to see her behind bars.

But everyone thought she was guilty.

"Hormones," the judge said as an aside to the clerk at the bail hearing, and the clerk nodded back to him.

I didn't think any amount of hormones were necessary to kill Bradford Blythe. He had been a royal bastard. After Bridget was released, Lucy and I brought her home, tucked her into bed, gave her a mug of hot chocolate, and handed her her laptop after she insisted that she needed to work.

"You've been training for this moment your whole life," Lucy told me as we sat on Bridget's bed, drinking hot chocolate.

"I have?"

"You're going to solve this mystery. You have to find the killer, and get the fuzz off of Bridget."

"Oh, would you do that, Gladie? That would make me so happy," Bridget said, smiling for the first time in hours.

I swallowed. "I'll try," I said. Normally, I would have

jumped at solving a mystery. But the pressure was terrible. What if I let Bridget down and she wound up in jail?

"You can do this," Lucy said. "And happy birthday, darlin'. I guess we'll have to celebrate later." She handed me a wrapped gift, which smelled strongly of an expensive perfume.

"Thank you, Lucy."

"It's French. Enjoy."

It wasn't until I was outside that I remembered that I didn't have a car, and it was too far to walk home. I was stuck, but I was also relieved to have a moment to myself, just me and the fresh air. So much had happened in the past couple days, and it was difficult to take stock. I took a deep breath and was thankful for it. There was a lot to do, a lot to think about, and I didn't know where to start. But it turned out that I wasn't going to have a lot of time to myself to think on that sidewalk. A car drove up and stopped in front of me.

The window opened and Ruth stuck her head out. "Get in, girl. The cavalry's here."

Her short hair framed her serious face. She projected a definite sense of purpose. "How did you know I was here?"

"How do you think? Your grandmother, of course. She made me put Julie in charge of Tea Time. Not that I had any customers. The whole town is hiding from Bridget and boiling their stupid-ass eggs."

I got into the car. "She told me I have to help you," Ruth continued. "Normally, I wouldn't listen to her. Third eye, my Aunt Fanny. And I don't give two hoots about her heart event. Do you know how many heart events I've had?"

"Five?"

"Three. This is only her first one. After my first one, I was back at Tea Time an hour later. So, I don't give a rat's patootie about her event."

"So why are you doing it?"

"Dementia, of course. It's the first sign."

She turned onto our street. "I don't think I need any help," I said, but I wasn't so sure. This was a big mystery with no suspects, and if I didn't solve it, my best friend would wind up in prison for the rest of her life.

"Holy moly, girl," Ruth said. "You got that look you get. Like you've got a tiger by the tail."

I didn't have a tiger by the tail. I didn't know who killed Bradford Blythe. I didn't even have a clue. But… "It's the weirdest thing, Ruth. The past couple days, I've gotten the feeling that everyone is lying to me. Like nothing is the way it seems."

It would take a lot of effort to take it apart and figure out where the truth lay. But one thing I knew was that I couldn't trust anyone.

"Being in the tea business for nearly a century, I can tell you that the minute you trust a person, you're doomed," Ruth said, wisely.

Ruth parked in the driveway, and we went into my grandmother's house. Thankfully, the egg people weren't there, but Bird had come to bring lunch for my grandmother and Meryl, and Grandma was sitting in the kitchen, out of bed for the first time since her heart event. I gave her a kiss.

"Sit down, Gladie," Bird said. "I brought enough for everyone. You're in for a treat. This 1950s diet is the best."

The table was set with a ham, mashed potatoes, overcooked green beans, and a pineapple upside down cake. Bird put a Jello mold onto the table as I sat.

"What the hell is this?" Ruth asked. "Am I having a flashback? If Eisenhower walks through the door, I'm killing myself."

"Shut up, Ruth," Bird said. "This is the 1950s diet. Nobody was fat in the 1950s. It was the good old days."

"Yeah, the good old days," Ruth grumbled. "Maxi pads six inches thick, girdles that cut you in half, and no women's rights. Perfect."

Despite her complaining, she was eyeing the ham intently,

and she licked her lips. She sat down and picked up her fork. "Hello, Zelda. How's the heart?" she asked.

"A little tired, but fine. Aching to get back to my matches, though. You know how it is to have a calling, Ruth."

Ruth nodded. "Tea's my life. Meryl, why do you have a bird on your shoulder?"

"I'm hoping that through closeness with me, he'll learn English again," Meryl said.

"Is that some kind of Jane Goodall thing?"

The food was delicious, but my thoughts were elsewhere. It was important to figure out why I was being lied to, and what the truth was. My first stop would have to be the scene of the crime.

"Have you ever heard of a body buried under the ceramic cat store, Grandma?" I asked.

"I have," Bird said, chewing ham. "I hear it's Jimmy Hoffa under there."

"I heard it was Moe McGregor, the miner that settled this town," Meryl said. "I heard that he was killed with a pick axe, and his gold nuggets were stolen."

"That's a *Bonanza* episode," Bird said, pointing her fork at Meryl.

My grandmother shrugged. "I know love, dolly. Not

murder."

It could have been a miner or Jimmy Hoffa, but I was wondering if it was someone more recent than that, or if it was nobody at all, and Liz Essex was lying to me. I did think she was lying, but not lying about a body. For some reason, she wanted me to know that somebody was buried there, and I didn't trust her motivation.

Looking at Ruth out of the corner of my eye, I noticed that she was being awfully quiet.

"I think I'll go over there after lunch," I said. Ruth smiled slightly. She would have loved an excuse to stir up trouble at Buckstars.

"You might make a match today, too," my grandmother said.

I sighed. Being employed was such a pain in the ass.

After lunch, I helped Bird wash the dishes, and Ruth helped Grandma go back to bed. Ruth and I met at her car afterward.

"Buckstars?" she asked me eagerly while she unlocked her car.

"Can you behave when you're there?"

"Gladie, they filled my dumpster with their corporate to-go cups, and that bastard Ford stole my Tea Time sign. I still haven't found it."

"An eye for an eye, Ruth. You weren't nice to their sign."

"Whose side are you on, girl? Choose wisely." She squinted at me, her face all wrinkles and droop. Her hair was severe with its short bowl cut. She was a fearsome woman.

"Yours," I chose.

I wasn't stupid.

We parked in front of Tea Time. Main Street was dead, probably because of the real death that happened a couple hours before. "How're we doing this?" Ruth asked me, as we stood on the sidewalk. "Good cop, bad cop? I'll be the bad cop. I've got a Yellow Pages inside. I could whack the bastard across the head with it. That'll make him talk."

"Good idea, but maybe we'll save the Yellow Pages for an emergency."

Ruth made a gun with her hand and shot me. "Gotcha."

"You know, maybe I should go in alone," I suggested.

"Nice try, Gladie. Your grandmother told me to stick with you."

Ruth never let anyone tell her what to do, let alone my grandmother, which meant she was using that as an excuse to harass the Buckstars owners. "Try to behave," I said.

"I'm eighty-six. What you see is what you get."

But I didn't have to worry about Ruth behaving because the door to Buckstars was locked and nobody answered when I knocked.

"Cowards," Ruth said. "They let a little murder shut them down. If you don't have the cajones for retail, you should get out now."

What was I going to do? I needed to investigate the scene of the crime.

"Look, Gladie," Ruth said, pointing. "It's the supermodel cop, and she doesn't look too happy to see you."

Sure enough, Terri was jaywalking across the street, and she already had her ticket book open. And she was writing in it.

"What now?" I whined.

"Loitering while annoying," Terri said. "Breaking and entering at a crime scene."

"I'm standing on the sidewalk."

"In Uggs. I'll write a ticket for that, too."

"What on earth did you do to her, Gladie?" Ruth asked. It was a fair question. Besides probably being responsible for her demotion, I hadn't done a damned thing. Now that I knew she wasn't in love with Spencer, but in love with Fred, I couldn't figure out why she hated me so much. It was making me crazy.

"Can't we be friends?" I asked Terri, and she grunted in response.

"What the hell?" Ruth asked, looking down the street.

It looked like a balloon was walking toward us, and it kept saying, "Ha-cha! Ha-cha!" and doing karate chops in the air.

"This town has more wackos then Bellevue," Ruth grumbled. "It's coming this way. You want me to get my Yellow Pages?"

Terri took a step backward. "It's like a rabid dog, but it's walking on two legs."

"It's a sumo wrestler," I breathed, rubbing my eyes because I couldn't believe what I was seeing. What were the odds?

"No, it's a woman dressed up like a sumo wrestler. It's one of those weird blow-up costumes," Ruth said.

The woman continued to shout, "Ha-cha! Ha-cha!" as she walked, karate chopping the air.

"It's coming at me in a threatening manner," Terri said, touching her holstered gun.

"I'll handle this for you," I told her, trying to be helpful and make her my friend.

I ran up to the sumo wrestler. Ruth was right. It was a woman, dressed in a large, balloon-like sumo wrestler costume.

"Hi," I started.

"Hi. Can't stop to chat. It's hard to balance in this thing. Ha-cha!"

"Sure thing," I said.

"I'm doing the sumo workout. I've gone down a half size already. Boy do I sweat in this thing. I do thirty minutes a day, but I have to keep walking. Otherwise, I fall over like a bowling pin."

"It's okay," I yelled back at Terri. "She's doing the sumo workout!"

"Stop in the name of the law!" Terri yelled at the sumo woman. Ruth stepped out of our path, but Terri planted her feet shoulder width apart, and her hand was still on her gun.

"So, do you cook?" I asked the sumo woman.

"That's my problem. I don't stop. What can I do? It's my method of meditation. So, I have to work out. I found this one during a commercial break when I was watching sumo wrestling on TV."

"Watching TV with your husband?" I asked.

"No, I'm single."

Ding. Ding. Ding. Could making a match be this easy? It was almost like it fell in my lap. Like a sumo wrestling fan cook walked into my life. We were getting closer to Terri.

"You should probably get out of the way," the sumo woman called to Terri. "I don't brake too well in this thing."

"Stop in the name of the law!"

I rolled my eyes. Being Terri's friend was a monumental task. "She has balance problems!" I warned Terri.

"I've heard that one before. What do you have hiding in that suit?"

The sumo woman started to sweat and then she started to wobble. If she kept going, she would run into Terri or get shot. "Hop off the sidewalk," I urged her. "There's no traffic. You'll be fine."

"Okay," she said. "This is only my third time doing the sumo workout. I'm sure I'll be better with more practice."

"I'm sure," I said. "She's going to walk on the street!" I called to Terri.

"Not on my street!"

I wanted to punch her in the face.

"It's like I'm watching the Titanic happen," Ruth said. "Or the Hindenburg."

She was right. It was a disaster about to happen. Any idiot could see that. With the added pressure and a gradual downward slant to the street, the sumo woman was seriously wobbling, now. A physically unfit and wholly uncoordinated woman in a sumo wrestling costume was going to go down like a ton of bricks, and nobody could stop it.

We were almost on top of Terri, and the moron wasn't moving. "Stop in the name of the law!" she yelled again.

"I don't know what to do!" the sumo woman yelled.

"Hop onto the street!" I said. "I'll help you!"

"Okay! I'm hopping!"

She hopped.

Sort of.

One foot landed, but the other foot was stuck for a split second on the sidewalk. "Hop! Hop!" I urged.

"I can't look away!" Ruth shouted.

"I'll help you!" I yelled at the sumo woman.

It was times like these that I wished I minded my own business. Nothing good came from being a Good Samaritan. As Ruth would say, no good dead went unpunished. I should have let the sumo woman ram into Terri and go on my way. Terri deserved it, for sure. But for the poor woman, who was desperate to lose weight and had donned an enormous sumo wrestling costume and ran down the street, I had to help. Besides, I was going to match her, and the number one rule in matchmaking was you couldn't match a dead person.

Like a ninja samurai, I flew into the air. Just as she was about to fall, I managed to grab hold of her hand.

"No!" she yelled.

Because she might have been fine if I hadn't helped her, and when I "helped" her, I might have knocked her off balance. Luckily, the costume was so wide around that she didn't hit her head when she hit the street. And luckily, there was no traffic. But it wasn't good luck that there really was a gradual downhill slant.

"Ooph!" she grunted as she toppled over onto the asphalt.

It was downhill from there.

She was just like Violet when she turned into a giant blueberry in *Willy Wonka*, except that she wasn't purple. "I don't like this!" she screamed and then she just screamed without saying anything.

"I'll help you!" I yelled, running after her. But she had a head start on me, and she was rolling faster than I could run.

"She's picking up speed!" Ruth yelled. "I'm having an LSD flashback! It's 1967 all over again! Someone save Bobby Kennedy!"

I ran full out after the poor sumo woman, who was screaming her lungs out.

"Let a law enforcement professional handle this," Terri said.

Terri Williams might have been a law enforcement

professional. She might have worked out five times a week and hadn't eaten a carbohydrate since she had reached puberty. But Terri Williams was no match for a chubby woman in a sumo wrestler costume, rolling down the street at fifteen miles an hour.

Karma. It's a bitch.

CHAPTER 10

I once had a match who proposed in a shark tank. That didn't end well. When proposing, tell your match: Nothing with teeth.

Lesson 37, Matchmaking advice from your Grandma Zelda

Miraculously, the sumo woman was unhurt, and she didn't hate me. I got her contact information, and she was over the moon excited at the prospect of a large man who was searching for a committed relationship. She decided being in shape was overrated, and I helped her out of her costume, which she threw in the trash can on the corner.

Terri wasn't so lucky. She had valiantly tried to stop the sumo woman, but she only managed to get knocked off her feet. She rolled the rest of the way down Main Street, wrapped around the sumo woman. She finally came to a stop, flat on her back, with her arm in the gutter.

"Get away from me," she croaked, as I bent over her, looking for signs of life.

"Are you all right?"

"I have asphalt in my mouth."

"At least you didn't shoot her. I think that shows admirable qualities of restraint."

"If I could move my arm, I would shoot you right here and now."

"I'll call an ambulance," I said.

"No. In the past couple of days, I've flown into a pole and gotten bitten by a woman. I'll never live down rolling through town with a sumo wrestler."

It was charmingly naïve of her to believe that word of the sumo wrestler wouldn't blow through town within an hour. It almost made me like her.

"You want me to help you?"

"Only if you kill yourself first."

She was a gorgeous woman, more beautiful than any model, but boy, she was a bitch. "You saved the day, Terri," I said. "A real law enforcement professional at work. I was in awe, watching you and your bravery."

Could a person die from bullshit? I hoped not.

"I really think we could be good friends," I continued. Now I wasn't believing me, either.

"I just want to get home to my cats," she mumbled.

"What was that? What'd you say?"

"Nothing."

But I had heard her. The supermodel had cats. I guessed the matchmaking gods were giving me birthday presents. I could match Terri with Bruce Coyle, and then she would get off Fred's back and off mine, too. But I would have to be smooth and clever to get the match done.

I rifled through my purse and took out Lucy's beautifully wrapped present. The scent of the expensive perfume permeated the box and the wrapping. "I got you a friendship gift," I lied to Terri. I was sure Lucy wouldn't mind me re-gifting her present if it got me a match and saved me a couple thousand dollars in tickets.

Terri's eye grew big. "You did? Perfume? I love perfume, but I don't wear it much. It smells expensive."

It was the nicest she had ever been to me, and in my mind, I patted myself on my back for my genius. I handed her the box. "For you," I said, sweetly.

She took the box with her good arm and clutched it to her

chest. "Go away."

"You don't want me to help you up?"

"Go away before I give you a ticket for trying to kill me."

"All righty," I sang and walked up the street to Ruth.

"For the first time, I wish I had a smartphone so I could have videoed that whole thing. I could have made a fortune on You Tube," Ruth said.

"I don't know why she doesn't like me."

"You don't?"

"That wasn't my fault. I wasn't rolling down the street," I pointed out.

"You knocked the poor woman down. You initiated the roll, Gladie. Admit it. You initiated the roll."

She was right, but there was no way I was going to admit it.

"I'm going to match the sumo woman," I said.

Ruth shook her head, like she pitied me. "What a way to make a living."

Since Buckstars was closed, we moved on to question the egg people. "What do those idiots have to do with a stranger's murder?" Ruth asked, as she drove us to Josephine's house.

"I don't know."

But I couldn't shake the feeling that they were involved. What had Josephine told me? She had once seen a dead person but didn't tell anyone. Could that be the person buried under Buckstars? Could she have been confessing something to me?

Josephine lived in a small cottage, just outside of the Historic District. When we arrived, I could smell the eggs before I got out of the car. "Josephine used to work on Wall Street," Ruth told me, as we walked up the front steps. "Her ex-husband was a hedge fund guy."

"Bradford Blythe was a venture capitalist," I said, noting the link.

"So, she stabbed him to death and then went home to boil eggs?" Ruth asked, suspicious. "Sounds reasonable."

I knocked on the door, and Josephine answered, letting out a cloud of steam. Her hair was even more of a frizzball than it was earlier in the day.

She smiled wide when she saw me. "Oh, Gladie. Thank you for coming and volunteering!"

"Uh," I said, as she pulled me into her house. Ruth followed. Every surface of Josephine's home was covered in hard-boiled eggs. Ruth pushed aside a couple dozen and sat on the couch.

"It's like D-Day in here, Josephine," Ruth said. "But D-Day was to stop the spread of fascism and beat the Nazis. Why are you doing this?"

"We're going to be in the Paramount World Record book, Ruth," Josephine said, proudly. She had turned the corner from Debbie Downer to full-throated participant. "We're putting Cannes on the map."

"It's on every map I've ever seen," Ruth said.

"Ruth Fletcher, when you die, your tombstone is going to read, *Party Pooper.*"

"No, it's not. It's going to read, *I Wasn't Dumb Enough to Boil a Hundred Thousand Eggs.*"

I stepped between them and gave Josephine my biggest smile. "How can I help, Josephine?" I heard myself ask. She showed me to her small kitchen where every pot was boiling at least a dozen eggs.

"You can drain," she said, like I knew what that meant.

"Crazy about today," I commented, picking up a pair of pot holders.

"Well, hormones combined with tax season made Bridget lose her mind. That's what everyone's saying."

That sounded pretty convincing to me. I would have to find out who the real killer was quick or Bridget was a goner. I picked up a pot and poured the boiling water into a strainer in the sink.

"Gently!" Josephine shrieked. "No cracking the eggs."

Wow, Easter was stressful. "Poor man, the man who was killed," I said, as I got a face full of steam.

"Yeah, I guess so."

My antennae stood up. She didn't sound torn up about the murder. "Did you know him?"

"Me? Of course not."

"He worked on Wall Street, too."

Josephine put her hands on her hips and pursed her lips. "A lot of people work on Wall Street, Gladie. I don't know all of them."

Defensive. Definitely defensive.

"Of course not." I picked up another pot.

"But I did know someone who knew him," she continued. I froze with the pot in my hands. "You won't tell a soul, will you?"

"Would I tell a soul?" I said like a question so it wouldn't be a lie.

"The owner of Buckstars. When the murdered guy walked in, the owner said, 'What are you doing here? I don't want any trouble.' What do you think of that?"

I thought I wished I could have gotten into Buckstars and grilled the Essexes. "Sounds interesting," I said.

"And then there's Bridget, of course," Josephine said. "I heard they were in business together. Funny business. Like maybe Bridget wasn't so honest with her numbers."

So, the baby daddy information hadn't gotten out. That was good. But I didn't like Bridget's professional reputation tarnished. "Bridget has only ever been honest with her numbers," I insisted. "She's the most trustworthy person I've ever met. The most trustworthy person you've ever met."

Josephine shrugged. "I'm just telling you what I heard."

I had come over to ask Josephine about something she had told me, and now she was defensive. That wouldn't make it easier to get information out of her. I needed her to be in a better mood.

"Have I mentioned how impressed I am with what you've done with the Easter egg hunt?" I asked her, kissing her butt. It worked. She blushed and flipped her frizzed out hair. "There are a lot of volunteers in this town, but none of them have tried to pull off something this big. I think the town should give you a volunteer award."

Her face brightened, and she stood up straighter. "You think so?"

"Oh, yes."

We talked for about twenty minutes about the minutiae of how to break a world record with eggs and how to mobilize an entire town toward a singular purpose. All the while, I boiled about a hundred eggs. My skin was dewy soft from the steam, and my makeup had melted off after five minutes.

"You know, Josephine," I said nonchalantly, leaning against her counter, when she was good and relaxed. "Call me silly, but I can't stop thinking about what you told me yesterday. You know, about finding a dead body. That's so exciting!"

"Really? You find a dead body ever week."

"Not every week. Maybe every month." I giggled like we were talking about nail colors. "Anyhoo… So, spill about the dead body. I promise I won't tell."

I crossed my fingers behind my back so I wouldn't go to hell.

"I don't know if I should," she said, her face a picture of fear.

"Oh, come on. What could it hurt?"

She smiled, as if she was pleased to dish the dirt. "Well, all right. You know, it's sort of strange because today reminded me of that day. You know, because it was in a weird place, not a place where you'd expect to find someone murdered."

Her phone rang, and she stuck a finger up. "This is my mother, Gladie. Can we finish this another time?"

No! Of course we can't finish this another time! My best friend is up for murder! Now, spill the beans, or I'm going to boil you like an Easter egg.

"No problem," I said, my mouth upturned in a frozen smile.

"Hi, Mom," she said into the phone and walked out of the kitchen, just as Ruth walked in.

"Well?" she asked me. "Can we leave now? I feel like I'm an old Jewish man taking a shvitz in Brooklyn."

"I'm pretty sure that's racist, Ruth."

"What's racist about Brooklyn?"

"I'm ready. Let's go."

"What did you find out?" she asked me as we left Josephine's house.

"Nothing. A big goose egg. Just that Ford Essex knew Brad, but I already knew that."

Ruth perked up. "You already knew that? Why didn't you tell me before? We need to get in that place, Gladie."

"I know."

We drove back to Buckstars. It was still locked, and the inside was dark. It was getting dark outside, too.

"What're we going to do?" Ruth asked me. "I know. We could kidnap them."

"Kidnapping is a federal charge."

"So is stealing mail. What's your point?"

I willed myself to be smart. Bridget was counting on me, and I was getting nowhere fast. "Okay, here's what we're going to do," I began, but I was interrupted.

"Pinky, I knew I would find you here."

It was the deep, velvety voice of Spencer Bolton. My boyfriend. The man who arrested my best friend for murder. He had changed his suit, and he was stunningly handsome. He smelled nice, too, and I instantly regretted giving away my fancy, expensive perfume.

"What are you doing here?" I asked, crossing my arms in front of me. "Did you run out of my friends to arrest?"

"We weren't doing anything we weren't supposed to," Ruth told him, crossing her arms, defiantly.

He arched an eyebrow. "I'm happy to hear that, Ruth. So, you couldn't find another sumo wrestler to throw at my cops?"

"I didn't throw her," I said.

"She didn't even push her on purpose," Ruth explained. "She was trying to help, and that stupid cop of yours got in the way."

"Interesting graffiti on the Buckstars sign," Spencer said. He gave Ruth the stink-eye.

"I better get going," Ruth said, avoiding any discussion of the *Fuckstars* sign. "Julie probably Superglued the teacups to the saucers again. Bye, Gladie. We'll talk about you know what tomorrow."

"Talk about what?" Spencer asked me when Ruth walked away.

"Why? You want to arrest Ruth, too?"

Spencer stepped forward and wrapped his arms around my waist, pulling me against him. "Pinky, I'm so sorry about Bridget. And I'm so sorry about your birthday. I know this will work out. In the meantime, let's celebrate another year. Let me take you to dinner."

I tried to harden myself against his barrage of hormones, but no way could I be that hard. Until they invented a hormone-proof vest to fend off his Superman pheromones, I was helpless. "Are you really taking me out for my birthday dinner, or is this a ruse to arrest me and take me to jail?"

"How long are you going to keep this going?"

"Forty years."

Spencer sighed. "Okay. That's fair. I thought you were going to hold a grudge. It's good to know you let things go."

"Let things go like letting Bridget go?"

"It's going to be a long forty years."

I lowered my head so he couldn't see that I was smiling. I was secretly tickled that he was thinking we would be together for forty years. What would we be like in forty years? Would we still like each other? Would he take me for granted? Would he expect me to wash the dishes and wash his underpants? It was overwhelming to think of being in a relationship for forty years, even if it was with Spencer.

"You okay, Pinky? You're breathing kind of hard."

"Fine," I lied. "I guess I'm hungry."

"That's the woman I know and love."

After we checked on my grandmother and I dressed in a pornographic red dress and heels, Spencer took me to the fanciest restaurant I had ever seen. It was high up in the mountains with a view for miles. Inside, the restaurant was decorated in white and black, and the waiters all spoke French.

"Monsieur Bolton?" the maître d' asked Spencer and walked us to a table next to the window.

The restaurant was so fancy that it didn't have menus. The waiter explained to us what we were about to eat in a long monologue. "I didn't understand a word he said," I told Spencer. "Half of it was in French and the other half was in science. I don't know either of those languages."

"Whatever it is, it's delicious," Spencer told me. "Even if we don't like it, it's delicious. You'd think they would give us a basket of bread, though."

An older man appeared at our table and opened a bottle of champagne, which he described in another long monologue. He poured two glasses and left the bottle in an ice bucket. Something about it triggered anxiety in me, but I didn't know why.

"To you," Spencer said, lifting his glass. I clinked my glass to his and took a sip.

Our first course arrived. I couldn't figure out what it was, but it tasted delicious. "This is even better than fish and chips," I said.

"Are you trying to poison me?" the man at the next table asked his waiter.

"No, monsieur. Of course not."

"Whatever I'm eating is gassy."

"No, we don't serve gassy."

"I'm telling you it's gassy."

"How about you?" I whispered to Spencer. "Is the food making you gassy?"

"Oh, Pinky. I love when you worry about me."

He took my hand and caressed my palm with his thumb. He drank me in with his eyes, and I was almost not angry at him anymore for arresting my best friend. "Pinky," he started, entirely serious and full of emotion.

"Yes?" I choked.

"The next course," the waiter began, interrupting us. I longed to be at Chik'n Lik'n, where they served the food in a bucket and forgot all about their diners. The waiter continued to talk a long time about duck, while Spencer didn't take his eyes off of me. I was warm all over, and I took another sip of champagne to cool off, but it only made me hotter.

Oh, mama.

The waiter stepped aside, and two young men served us our second course at the same time, as if they were synchronized swimmers. Then they stepped back, and I half-expected them to sing, "ta da!" But they simply turned around and walked away, leaving Spencer and me at our candlelit table with our gourmet food.

"Have I told you how beautiful you are tonight?" Spencer asked me. His eyes flicked to my breasts and returned to my face. He smirked his little smirk.

"I don't think you mentioned it." I was having a hard time breathing. It was all I could do not to swipe the dishes off the table, jump on it, and pull Spencer on top of me. It felt like Spencer was using the fancy dinner as a lead up to something big, and I wasn't sure if it was sex in the car or something more *Leave it to Beaver.* Whichever it was, I was getting nervous and excited.

Slightly less nervous and more excited about the sex in the car, though, than *Leave it to Beaver.*

I took an absentminded stab at my second course with my fork and missed my mouth on the way up. "I paid a lot of money for this stuff, and it's gassy!" the man at the next table grumbled to his wife.

"Don't blame the food for your gas, Marvin," his wife said with her mouth full.

"My appetizer was fifty-five dollars, and I've got a gut full of gas."

"So sue me if I'm trying to keep our romance alive. Prince Charming never told Snow White that he was gassy."

"You're no Snow White, Blanche."

I re-focused on Spencer. He was eating slowly, his attention still riveted on me. "Obviously, my life hasn't been the same since I met you," he said. Spencer had met me when I was hanging upside down from a telephone pole with my pants pulled off. I was waiting for his punchline about how wacky his life is with me in it, but he had different ideas than teasing me. "I think I only became alive when you came into my life. I can't imagine you not in it. Every morning that I wake up with you next to me, I wonder what good deed I've done to be rewarded like this. This thing we have is so good. There's passion and more than that. There's friendship."

Whoa. I was really turned on. My insides were hot and melting. I felt feverish. My face must have been bright red.

But I still wanted to make a snarky comment about him arresting my friend.

I took a sip of champagne.

"Go on," I croaked. "You're doing good."

Spencer leaned forward. "I think we need to go to the next level."

"Anal? You know how I feel about that."

He blinked. "No. Not that. I mean, the next level in our relationship."

I gulped back the rest of my champagne and adjusted my boobs in my dress. "I don't know about relationship levels. What level are we on now?"

Spencer smirked. "You're sweating, Pinky. Relationship talk freaks you out."

He was right. Relationship talk freak me out. Freaked me out more than taxes but less than spiders. "That's not true," I said.

"I'm a mature, responsible woman. I'm not afraid of relationships. Is there more champagne?"

He poured me another glass. "I'm committed to you, Pinky," he continued. "I'll always be there for you."

"You will?"

Nobody had ever been there for me always, except for my grandmother.

Spencer took my hand. "Always," he said, his voice full of emotion.

And then it happened. The moment I had been waiting for and fearing for weeks. With his other hand, Spencer put a little box onto the table.

A ring box.

A red ring box.

The crazy thought that flashed through my head was that the box matched my dress. *If a ring box matches my dress, does that mean that I have to say yes?* That was my crazy thought.

"I love you, Pinky," he said and slid the box over to my side of the table. I stared at it, like I was expecting a troop of clowns to come out of it.

"I wish I knew that I should have brought Maalox to a place like this," the man at the next table said.

"Marvin, I'm pretending you don't exist. I'm going to eat my elk tenderloin and ignore you completely," his wife said.

"With the food this gassy, I doubt you'll be able to ignore me for long, Blanche."

I opened the ring box.

"What's this?" I asked.

"Do you like it?" Spencer asked, bouncing in his chair, like he was five years old.

"I don't know much about fashion."

"It's a key. I don't think it has any fashionable use, Pinky."

I held it up and studied it. It wasn't a ring. I double checked the box. Nope. No ring. "It's a key," I repeated.

Spencer let go of my hand and sat back in his chair. "It's a key to the house across the street from your grandmother's house."

"The cursed house?"

"It's not cursed."

"Murders and a plane crash. That spells cursed to me."

"Pinky, you and I both know that you're a terrible speller."

I put the key back in the box. "I know how to spell cursed."

"The house has had some bad luck. That means it's only going to have good luck from now on."

I harrumphed and crossed my legs. The waiter returned to our table.

"For your next course, we have pheasant flown in from Madagascar," he started.

"Good for them. You wouldn't think a little bird could fly that far," I said to the waiter.

"I know what this is about," Spencer continued. "You don't want to live with me. It's fine if we play sleepover and it's your room in your house. Your territory. But you don't want to set up house *with* me. You don't want to be *with* me. You don't want any kind of *with*."

"I have nothing against *with*," I insisted.

"I just gave you a house, and you're throwing it back at me."

"No, you gave yourself a house and assumed that I would live there with you and do your laundry and iron your shirts."

"Pinky, I'm not insane. I wouldn't trust you with my shirts."

"And I wouldn't trust you not to arrest my best friend. My best friend!"

"The elk tenderloin is also a fine choice if you don't like

pheasant," the waiter said.

"Don't get the elk tenderloin," the man at the next table warned me. "Very gassy."

"Stay out of this," Spencer growled.

"Or he'll arrest you," I told the man. "He likes to arrest people for no reason."

"I arrest people when they're supposed to be arrested," Spencer yelled, throwing his napkin down on the table.

"Like Bridget would kill anyone. Like Bridget would take a knife and stab someone!"

"She was there, alone. She was holding the murder weapon, covered in blood!"

"She was trying to help him! She's pregnant! She's a single mother!"

"Well, now we're to the point. That was her decision. She decided to hide her little secret from the father."

"Father. Yeah right," I said.

"I know you think you're Miss Marple, but this is what I do for a living. You need to prepare yourself for the inevitable truth that your friend got angry and lashed out, and the result was a dead man."

My eyes widened, and my nostrils flared. "You take that

back."

"See, Blanche? Even the good-looking couples fight," the man at the next table said.

"Shut up!" I shouted at him.

"Don't you talk to my husband like that. He has a sensitive stomach," Blanche said.

To prove her point, her husband let it rip and farted. His fart sounded like a fog horn. "Excuse me," he said. "I told you the food was gassy."

"I don't care about your gassy food!" I shouted. I stood up. "Don't follow me," I told Spencer. "I'll call for a car. I don't want to see you."

I marched outside, and Spencer didn't follow me. I was dizzy and disoriented. I didn't know what had just happened, but I felt lost. No. I felt like I had lost. Lost everything.

And I would never be happy again.

CHAPTER 11

Love conquers all? Not every time, bubbeleh. There will be a time where you have a match, and the match is working. It looks like they're heading toward their happy ending. And then it all goes to hell. All is lost. Or is it? Maybe not, dolly! Maybe not! Sometimes you can pull it back from disaster. Like fixing a bad meal, add some schmaltz to it. Schmaltz makes everything taste better.

Lesson 53, Matchmaking advice from your Grandma Zelda

I was home fifteen minutes later. I had cried my makeup off. My grandmother's room was dark, so I didn't stop in to see her. Quietly, I went into my room and closed the door. I threw my dress in the corner of my room and put on sweats, a T-shirt, and thick socks.

"Men are all the same," I muttered to myself, while the tears streamed down my face. "They wait until I love them, and then they show their true selves." But Spencer was the only man I had ever truly loved. And he would probably be the only man I would ever love.

Because what are the odds of finding two Mr. Rights in a lifetime?

There was nobody on earth like Spencer. Sure, he was a frat boy, womanizing, cartoon-watching, baseball fanatic. But he was also…well, he was everything.

The bastard.

I sat on my bed, hugging my knees to my chest, and I replayed in my head every stupid word I had uttered during our fancy, romantic dinner. He had bought me a house. A big, real house across the street from my grandmother so that I would never be far from her. And the house had a pool.

I now owned a pool.

I tried to let that sink in. A pool. A house. Me.

Spencer told me that he would be there for me always. What was a better sign of always than brick and mortar? A house that could withstand a plane crash could withstand the likes of Spencer and me.

But I threw his always back into his face, crumbling the brick and mortar into dust. I was more destructive than a plane crashing into it. I had rejected Spencer, rejected his gift, rejected his promise.

I blew my nose on my pillowcase.

What kind of woman was I? I was a terrible person. He had bared his soul to me, and I had yelled at him for arresting Bridget.

But he shouldn't have arrested Bridget. It was ridiculous to think that she was capable of murdering someone, even if that someone was threatening to take away her child. Of course, I would have killed someone if they threatened to take away my child. I would have picked up the nearest knife and plunged it into his chest.

Oh.

Uh oh.

No. She couldn't have. She was Bridget. Human rights freak, not a cold-blooded murderer.

No. She didn't murder Bradford Blythe. It was unthinkable. She had total respect for humanity and the individual. She had spent her life, devoted to making lives better. So, no matter how she had been threatened, she wouldn't have reacted violently. I was sure of it.

I had to save her. I was determined to find the killer fast and prove her innocence. But I could understand how someone who thought they were a law enforcement official could have mistakenly believed that Bridget was the murderer. After all, she was holding the murder weapon. After all, she was being threatened by the murder victim. Motive, means, and opportunity.

Oh, Spencer.

Amateur.

I knew better. I knew that murder was never easy, never what it seemed. It was a rookie mistake to go for the obvious when solving a mystery. And something told me deep inside me that everything obvious with this mystery was a lie.

It was frustrating, and I was worried about Bridget. So, I had taken it out on Spencer, which wasn't fair.

But if I was going to be really honest with myself, that's not why I had gotten angry at him. If I was going to be truthful, my anger started with the key. Something about the key triggered my anger. Why did I get angry about a gift of a house and a promise to be together forever?

Because the always Spencer was promising me wasn't the always that I had dreamed of.

Could that be it? I had wanted more?

I gasped with the epiphany.

"No, that can't be it," I said out loud in my bedroom. "That can't be why I was angry. I don't want more than what he's offering."

What was he offering? A committed relationship with me, living in a house across the street from my grandmother. That was a lot.

But something inside me didn't trust it. It wasn't enough.

I wanted…

I wanted…

No, it couldn't be true.

Yes, it was.

I wanted to marry Spencer Bolton.

"Holy shitballs. Holy mother-lovin' shitballs. Holy The-Way-We-Were shitballs. Holy Doctor Zhivago, Romeo and Juliet, Here Comes the Bride shitballs."

The truth was that I had wanted the red ring box to be an engagement ring. Diamond, ruby, Cracker Jacks, I didn't care what kind of ring, but I wanted him to propose. I wanted to walk down an aisle or stand up in court or wherever we could exchange our vows to always be there for each other.

Damn it. What a moment for my commitment phobia to hit the road.

"I want to marry Spencer," I whined into my snotty pillow and cried. It was a growing up moment for me, and I was terrible at growing up moments. But I was having one, nonetheless. I wanted to marry Spencer, but I had sabotaged our relationship, and now it was over, and I would never see him, again.

Then, everything changed. The nerves on the back of my neck came to life, and like a wind vane when the wind changes, I shot up from bed and looked around. With total certainty, I knew that Spencer was close. "Spencer," I breathed.

I ran out of my room and took the stairs two and a time. I couldn't get to the front door fast enough. When I reached it, I flung it open and ran outside.

There he was. Spencer was standing in the driveway, looking up at my grandmother's house. He saw me, and we ran toward each other, as if we were in a movie. He grabbed me hard and kissed me like he never wanted to let me go.

Our tongues touched, our mouths crashed against each other. We kissed forever, unable to get enough. My body was on fire, but the kiss was more than sensual. As it continued, my heart filled up, knowing that we were together. It was real, no matter what happened.

The kiss finally ended and he cradled my face in his hands. "I thought I lost you. I was so stupid. I'm such a moron."

"I know."

He arched an eyebrow and smirked his little smirk. "In Gladie speak, that means you forgive me, right?"

"There's nothing to forgive. I need you to forgive me. I was the jerk. I'm such a jerk."

"I know."

I smiled. "In Spencer speak, that means I'm hot and you love me, right?"

"Right."

"So, would you give me the box, again? I'm ready for it, now."

"Are you sure?" he asked. "I don't want to push you."

"I've never been a homeowner before. And a pool owner. Can you believe I have a pool?"

"Well, right now it's a putrid, plastered cesspool, but yes, you own a pool. Here you go," he said, handing me the box.

In the light of the porch light, the box looked blue, instead of red.

"It's blue," I said. "I thought the box was red."

"It's blue. This is a different box. I was going to give this one to you after the one with the key in it."

My heart stopped. There wasn't one *thump thump* happening in my chest. The blue box was completely unexpected.

"You had this with you at the restaurant?" I asked.

"I brought two birthday presents for you." Spencer's voice was soft and low in his throat, as if he was nervous and choosing his words with care. "The key and this."

I held the box in my hand, feeling the weight. "Is it another key?"

"The key to my heart, Pinky." I opened the box. "It took me a long time to find it," he explained. "I didn't think a hunk of diamond was really you. But I thought this was you. It's vintage from the 1920s. A sapphire to match your eyes, circled with small diamonds. I stole one of your rings to get this one sized. It should fit you. Should I put it on your finger?"

I nodded because I couldn't get my vocal cords to work. Spencer pocketed the box and slipped the ring on the third finger of my left hand. It fit perfectly. I loved the ring. It was exactly my style.

"What does this mean?" I asked.

"It means that I get a man cave in our house."

"And I never wash your clothes," I said.

"And baseball season is sacrosanct."

"And you never arrest my friends, again. And we order takeout every night. And we get one of those fancy beds that can be adjusted up and down. And you'll be in charge of the trash. And we'll have a landline because I always have problems with my cellphones. And wood floors everywhere except for the bedrooms."

"I agree."

"You do?"

"Yes, carpet in the bedrooms."

"Okay," I said, studying my ring. "I guess we're getting married."

"Who said anything about marriage?" he asked. I punched him in the arm. "Love taps. Very sexy. Will you marry me, Pinky?"

"I'll marry you, Spencer."

"Good. I'm going to bang your brains out in the bushes. Married people do that, you know."

He swept me up in his arms and walked onto the lawn. "Be careful of the roses," I warned him. "Grandma will kill me if we damage them."

"Trust me, I'll avoid the roses when I'm naked."

"Oh, naked," I giggled. "I like you naked."

He got naked very fast. And he got me naked very fast. "Oh my God, Spencer," I said, looking at his shlong. "Did you take a pill? Or ten pills?"

"This is what you do to me. This is me as a marriage kind of man."

Spencer as a marriage kind of man was very impressive. Aggressive. Having sex in the front yard behind the bushes was naughty, but it was late, and the neighbors were all tucked into their homes. Spencer laid me on the grass, and nestled his mouth between my legs. "Oh, Spencer," I moaned. He tasted me, and I writhed against his talented tongue. I combed my fingers through his hair, and my mouth dropped open. "Ohhhhhh," I moaned. I was singing, again. Opera this time. Owning a house and a precious gem had made me a classy opera singer.

We flipped over, and I straddled him, carefully slipping him inside me. "Oh, Pinky," he moaned. It was his time for moaning. Normally, he was a quiet lover, but I guessed the marriage kind of man Spencer was loud.

Because he was being loud.

"Ohhhhh!" he moaned, as I went up and down.

"Look at this!" a familiar voice said, interrupting Spencer and me. A bright light shined on my face and my naked breasts. I stopped moving, and Spencer stopped moaning.

"Terri?" I asked, shielding my eyes and trying to see past the light.

"Indecent exposure!" Terri announced with unabashed glee at catching me in a true infraction instead of just being annoying. But she didn't seem to realize the extent of it, that I wasn't just naked, but that I was having sex with her boss in the bushes. "Naked outside. Oh, this is a good one!"

She lowered her flashlight, and I could see that she was writing another ticket.

"Naked boobies in a residential district," she continued, laughing.

"Naked everything, Terri," I said.

"Huh?"

She shined her light again, and this time she saw the whole thing: Me on top of Spencer, and Spencer angrier than spit.

"Oh, hello, Chief," she said, amiably, still not catching on. Then, she did. "Oh, hello chief," said with more of a tinge of horror in her voice.

"Turn off the flashlight. Now," he growled in his best boss voice as he laid flat on his back.

She turned it off. "I'm sorry, Chief. I didn't know that…well…"

"Leave. Now," he commanded.

"I… okay… well… I… okay… well…" She was stuck in a loop, probably from the shock of seeing her boss getting banged while she was on her rounds.

"Now," he growled. "I'd get up, but I'm indisposed. So, I would appreciate it if you would leave."

"Okay… bye… I…" It took her a good three minutes to get herself together enough to turn around and leave.

"She's traumatized," I said when she finally left. "She'll

probably have nightmares. At least your nakedness was covered up by my nakedness."

"I was so close when she interrupted us. Now, I'm a wet noodle. She's probably going to sue me."

"She's in love with Fred," I told him.

"I know. Hiring her was a huge lapse in judgment. I mean, who would ever fall in love with Fred?"

"Do you really think she'll sue you?"

"Absolutely. Her boss was having sex in front of her. I'm toast."

"I'll fix it," I said.

"Oh, God, Pinky. Please don't fix anything."

"I'm going to match her. I have a perfect match in mind. Then, she'll be happy and leave Fred alone and you alone." And me alone. I still didn't think it was smart to let Spencer know about my involvement with the couch or the biting.

"At least you haven't lost your optimism," he said. "Come on, let's take this party inside. Did you notice that Terri smelled really good?"

Yes. She was wearing my birthday present perfume. That was a good sign, as far as I was concerned.

We gathered our clothes, and Spencer's phone rang. "Chief

Bolton," he answered. "Uh huh. Uh huh. Are you kidding me? Uh huh. Okay. I'll be right there."

He hung up. "What's wrong?" I asked.

"Aliens."

I went to bed while Spencer went out on his aliens police call. It was hard to fall asleep because I was euphoric, and I was wearing a pretty ring. I was desperate to call Lucy and Bridget and tell them the news, but I didn't want to rub my good news in Bridget's face, now that she was being accused of murder, and if I told Lucy, she would have come over to get all the details, and I wouldn't get any sleep.

So, I laid in bed and stared at my ring in the light of the clock. After a long time of insomnia due to happiness, I fell asleep. Spencer woke me up when he came to bed a little before dawn.

"Look at my ring," I told him, shoving my hand in his face.

"Beautiful," he said, kissing my hand. He turned over and pulled the covers over him.

"What happened? Did the aliens call home?"

"No. Remember Urijah? Our contractor?"

The man who met with Bradford Blythe. How could I forget?

"He's an alien?" I asked.

"No. He saw an alien. There was a bright light, and when he went outside, his pet goat had been murdered."

"He has a pet goat?"

"Not anymore. This is a crazy-ass town. I'm the damned chief of police. I'm not supposed to go out on alien calls."

"Was the goat stabbed?"

"Pinky, I got to get some sleep," he said and started to snore. He was already in a deep sleep. But I was now wide awake. A murdered goat. I couldn't help but think that it had something to do with Brad's murder and that his murder was more complicated than everyone believed.

CHAPTER 12

Matchmaking is just like making coffee. Ask anyone how they like their coffee, and they'll say: Strong! Dark! Robust! But if you look through their kitchen window and spy on them at home, you'll see the truth. Their favorite coffee is pishachs. Weak as pee-pee. Full of milk and sugar. They say they want it strong and bitter, but they want it weak and sweet. So, trust your instinct, dolly. Don't trust your match.

Lesson 122, Matchmaking advice from your Grandma Zelda

The goat had been stabbed. Urijah told Spencer that the aliens were after its brain. Why aliens would come millions of miles to our planet just for a goat's brain, I had no clue. That's all the information I got out of Spencer before he went to work. I had a million questions and no answers. But first things first. I had matches to match.

I had already eaten breakfast with my grandmother, a long breakfast where we looked at my ring and didn't speak about the consequences and meanings of a precious gem and sliver of gold borne by a finger for what was supposed to be forever.

Afterwards, I had gotten dressed. "Gladie," Grandma called from her room. I picked up my purse to see what she needed before I left for the day. "First things first," she told me when I walked into her room.

"Matchmaking. I've got it covered," I said.

"You'll have to hold her hand for this one."

"Terri might not like that. So, I called Bruce, and I set up the meet so she won't know it's me."

"Smart! Matchmaking for the reluctant match. I told you that you have the gift." She patted the place on the bed next to her, and I sat down. She took my hand, the other hand where there was no ring. "Spencer is a good man. He's a mensch," she said.

I felt my face get hot.

"This is a good match," Grandma continued. "This is a true love match. A forever match."

"Forever's a long time, Grandma."

"I wish."

Bruce Coyle, pesticide truck driver and searcher for love, was thrilled that I had found him a match so quickly. "She looks like a model, and she loves cats," I told him. I decided to leave out the part about her being a bitch and in love with another man. I gave him a copy of her work picture off the internet. He approved heartily. Why wouldn't he? She was gorgeous.

Luckily, Tuesday was Terri's day off. It was the perfect time to send Bruce to her house under false pretenses. Sometimes love was a dirty business and a little underhanded. I met Bruce around the corner from Terri's house. "Here you go," I said, handing him a kitten that I had gotten from the shelter. "You know what to do."

The cat was orange and tiny. It was the kind of kitten Twitter followers watched in videos to reduce stress. I wasn't a huge cat lover, but even I was tempted to take the kitten home. Terri would be a goner.

"Oh, what a cute guy," Bruce said. "Hello, Mr. Orange, I'm Bruce. Wanna come home with me?"

"You know the plan, Bruce?" I asked.

"Yes, ma'am."

"Okay. This should go without a hitch. I have to leave on other business. You'll be okay, right?"

"Yes, ma'am."

Bruce was calm under pressure, not like the sumo wrestler who had freaked out on the phone when I gave him his match's contact information, like a man who was one step away from happiness but was afraid of stepping. But I had done it. I had made two matches in record time. If they didn't screw it up, I was free to find the killer and save Bridget. I patted myself on the back for filling in for my grandmother with amazing success. Maybe she was right and I really did have the gift.

I drove to Tea Time and parked in front. Buckstars had reopened, and there was a new sign that Ruth hadn't gotten to, yet. I walked into Tea Time, which had more people than the day before, but business was still lighter than normal.

"There you are," Ruth said, rushing me as I entered. "Time's a wasting. We have investigating to do."

"May I have a latte, please?"

"Here," she said, handing me a to-go cup. "I've got Julie filling in for me, but we don't have a lot of time. She's been worried about Fred, and she's distracted. She almost poisoned one customer already."

Ruth had a twinkle in her eye, the kind of twinkle that Charles Manson had probably been more than a little familiar with. There was no doubt in my mind that she was using this investigation as a means of torturing her new competition.

"Maybe I should go in alone," I suggested, taking a step

back, out of her reach. "Maybe they'll be more talkative that way." And less of a chance that Ruth and I would get arrested.

"Don't worry about me. I got this covered. I know just what to do."

"You're not going to kill them with your baseball bat, are you?"

"Not in the next five minutes."

"I can't go in there with your coffee," I said, taking a sip of my latte.

"Drink fast. Is that what I think it is?" she asked, eyeing my ring.

I blushed. "Yes." I braced myself for the onslaught of teasing.

"Good," she said, surprising me. "The cop's a good choice. A little too pretty for my taste, but he's got a steady job, and he looks at you like you're the melting Velveeta cheese in a Philly cheesesteak."

"Is that good?"

"It's better than a kick in the pants."

She had a point. It was better than a kick in the pants. And that's what a successful marriage was. It wasn't the state of euphoria that I was in, that moment when all the possibilities were presented but none of the struggles. But something told me that with all the struggles included, a marriage to Spencer would be better than a kick in the pants. Much better.

So, I agreed to let Ruth go with me to Buckstars, and I braced myself for the worst. I gulped half of my latte and handed her back the to go cup to throw away.

As Ruth and I walked into Buckstars, she whispered to me, "If this goes south, I'll flood the place, and you run for your life."

"We're just going to ask them some questions and look around. This isn't Da Nang in the sixties."

She harrumphed. "It's always Da Nang, Gladie. Always."

To my big surprise, Ruth plastered a big, unnatural smile on her face. "Look at this lovely establishment," she gushed loudly. There was more than one stunned face in Buckstars as Ruth entered. There was also a tangible rise in anxiety. "So clean! Very clean! Who would have ever thought to turn a coffee house into a surgical theater. Ingenious! Is that you, Ford? My, you look nice today."

Ruth was terrible at being phony, probably because she had had such little practice doing it. I snuck past her and made a beeline for the room in the back where the murder had taken place. The door was closed, and I opened it, walking inside.

It had been cleaned. There was no sign that anything nefarious had happened there. I searched for any clue, any sign of who had killed Bradford Blythe and why. Nothing.

"Hi, Gladie," I heard behind me, and I turned. It was Ford Essex, the owner of Buckstars. "Did you get lost on your way to the restroom?"

Normally under these circumstances, I had experienced that honesty was the worst policy. But for some reason, this time around, I decided to tell the truth.

"No. I was looking at the scene of the crime. You know, for clues."

I searched his face for signs of guilt. After all, the crime happened in his shop, and the way he had looked at Brad made it obvious that he knew him. But there were no signs of guilt on Ford Essex's face. In fact, he looked like he had never felt guilty in his life. But he probably should have. Because he was looking at me like a predator looks at his prey, or how I looked at a bologna sandwich. I took a step backward.

"You like true crime, huh?" he asked, giving me a come-hither look, which made me throw up a little in my mouth.

"Yes." It was sort of the truth. I wasn't a fan of true crime TV or books, but I had developed an obsession with real life real crime on more than one occasion. "Any ideas about what happened here?"

"That pregnant woman with the big glasses knifed the jerk a lot of times. Why? Have you heard something different?"

He took a couple steps forward, invading my personal space. I was getting a strong man-in-the-park-in-a-raincoat vibe off of him, and I took note of how many steps it was to escape from the small room. I also noted that the noise level wasn't that bad in the coffee shop, and if I screamed, I would probably be heard. Add to that the fact that Ruth would have loved any excuse to pound Ford's head in like she was tenderizing steak, I wasn't scared, no matter how grossed out I was by Ford's intense study of my breasts.

"I think the jury's out about the pregnant woman being the killer," I said. "I'm pretty sure the police are looking elsewhere," I lied. "There might have been a witness."

Oh, geez. I was such a good liar. The lies flowed out of me without me even thinking about them first. It was kind of like a muscle spasm of the mouth.

It was a good lie, and it did the trick. Ford took a step back, and his expression changed from leering to slight fear.

"Are you saying I did it?"

Yes, that's what I was saying. If he did it, I could save Bridget.

"Because I didn't do it," he continued, dashing my hopes for a confession. "I hated the bastard, but only an idiot would stab a man to death in his back room at his grand opening. You know what I mean?"

I knew what he meant, but I was hoping he was idiot enough to do just that.

"You hated the bastard?" I asked.

"Did I say that?"

"You mentioned it."

"Well, between you and me, I might have been in a small business venture with him last year, and it didn't go so well."

I remembered the look on Ford's face when he realized that Brad was in his shop. "And he had come back to be a bastard to you? Something about your small business venture?"

"I don't know why he was here. I didn't have a chance to ask him."

That could have been true or a lie. While I had been stuck in the crowd, I didn't see where Ford was. He could have snuck to the back room or not.

"I wouldn't blame you if you killed him," I said, trying to get him to confess.

"You would like that? Does that turn you on?"

Ew. I didn't know how to answer. If I said, yes, I was afraid where the conversation would lead, but if I said, no, I wouldn't get any further in getting him to spill the beans.

"You know, Liz and I are having our weekly key party tonight at seven. We would love to have you join us. You can bring your significant other, if you have one."

My thumb touched the ring on my finger, and I remembered that I did have a significant other. "Sure," I said. If

Spencer went with me, I wouldn't have to worry about being murdered or raped. Ford gave me his address. "I'm so happy you'll be joining us," he said, and leered at me.

Blech.

I hadn't gotten him to confess, but maybe at a party after a few drinks, he would spill his guts.

"What the hell is going on in here? Did you kidnap her?" Ruth demanded, storming into the room like a geriatric bulldog. She looked me over, as if she was searching for damage.

"We were just getting to know each other," Ford told her. "You don't mind staying out front where we can see you, do you? We don't want a replay of what you did to our back door."

"I was just going for a whiz. My bladder's older than Mount Rushmore, you know."

"I'll make sure she behaves," I told Ford.

"Just make sure you don't," he whispered to me and touched my chin. Ruth and I watched him leave the room.

"That man is walking herpes," Ruth said. "He's toe fungus. He's a booger that just won't go away."

"I think he might have killed Brad, but I can't prove it," I said. "He invited me to his key party tonight, and I'm going to grill him there."

"His key party? You're going to a key party?"

"Why is that so crazy? I have keys, you know, Ruth. I have a key to my grandmother's house and one to my car and one on my key ring that I have no idea what it goes to but I'm afraid to throw away."

Ruth crossed her arms in front of her. "Do you know what a key party is, girl?"

"A party with keys?" It did sound strange. I had no idea why keys made a party.

"The sixties, Gladie. The sixties. Each woman drops their key into a bowl, and later each man fishes one out, blindly, and goes home with the owner of the key. This explains so much. The Essexes are swingers."

"Swingers?"

"Swingers. His Donkey Kong is climbing every woman's Empire State, and her Happy as a Clam is saying how do you do to every man's Eiffel Tower."

"I'm so confused, Ruth. I was never good at geography."

She ignored me and snapped her fingers, as if she was Benjamin Franklin and had discovered electricity. "No wonder I was getting a stink off of them. Their whosits and whatsits are doing the cha-cha all over town. No wonder their coffee tastes like ass."

"The Essexes are swingers?" I asked, again.

"And they want to swing with you and Spencer, Gladie," Ruth continued. "Key party. Your key. He wants your key in his keyhole or vice versa. You want that? A little Ford Essex action in your keyhole?"

I shuddered. "Gross," I said. "I don't want to swing. I just got the ring. I'm very definitely not a swinger. My Happy as a Clam is happily monogamous. I'm only climbing Spencer's Eiffel Tower. Are you sure about them? They don't look like swingers. They look like insurance salesmen from the seventies."

"Pay attention. This makes complete sense. People coming and going at all hours at this place. The dead body under the floor. Those two are up to no good. I wouldn't be surprised if they killed Bradford Blythe and someone else besides. I mean, have you heard from Ethel since she sold this place to them?"

"No," I breathed, even though I had never spoken to Ethel in my life. If I could prove they killed Ethel, it would shine a light on them and away from Bridget.

"We have to dig up that body, Gladie."

"We have to dig up that body," I agreed. "Wait a minute. You drank coffee here?"

Ruth pursed her lips and nodded, curtly. "I'm lulling them into a false sense of security."

"That's taking one for the team."

"You're telling me."

Then, I saw it. Cradled in the grout between the floor tiles, there was a fingernail. I squatted down and looked more closely. It was an acrylic nail that was painted white, but there was a splash of red on it. Blood.

I picked it up and showed it to Ruth. "It's Liz Essex's fingernail," I said. "I would bet money on it." But it wasn't proof of anything. Even if it was Brad's blood on the nail and Liz was the murderer, she could have explained it away saying she had cleaned the room.

"Meet me at Tea Time at seven," Ruth instructed me. "I have a way in here. We'll dig up the body, and those corporate devils will get their due."

"Seven tonight?"

"Either that, or you can go to your wife swapping party."

"I'll see you at seven, Ruth."

Luckily, Spencer was working late, and Grandma had a friend staying with her. The egg people were in their homes, boiling, and my two matches were on dates. I was free to break and enter and break, again. But I didn't want to be alone with Ruth, especially since she had a personal vendetta against Buckstars and its owners and probably had access to noxious chemicals. So, I called Lucy and asked her to meet me at Tea Time at seven.

"Should I wear my black outfit, again, darlin'? Is it one of those kinds of meetings?"

"Yes," I said. "And bring all the night vision goggles you can find."

When six-thirty came around, I left the house and walked to Tea Time. I was dressed all in black, and I made it to the tea shop without anyone seeing me. Tea Time was dark, and the door was locked. I knocked, and Ruth opened it, immediately, letting me in. She was dressed in black, too.

"I can't wait until that Buckstars is dead and gone," she said, smiling wide.

"I hope we can clear Bridget's name."

"Yeah, that too," she said, vaguely.

The door opened, again, and Lucy walked in with her husband, Uncle Harry. Lucy was back in her black, designer outfit, and Harry was in a pinstripe suit. "Hey there, Legs," he said to me. "I hear we're robbing a bank."

"We're digging up a body," Ruth said. "But you weren't invited."

"I invited him, Ruth," Lucy said. "So, jump back."

"Fine. I guess we could use some more muscle."

"Oh, I brought muscle. Don't worry about that." Uncle Harry said.

"And I brought enough night vision goggles," Lucy said and handed them out.

Ruth slipped hers on over her head. "Good thinking. Someone help me with the jackhammer."

"You have a jackhammer?" I asked.

"Never robbed a bank with a jackhammer before," Harry said.

"We're digging up a body," I said.

"Never done that, either."

Ruth signaled to Harry to help her with her jackhammer, which was leaning against a table.

"Ruth, we can't use a jackhammer," Lucy explained in her patient Southern belle voice. "We'll wake the dead with that thing. We need to get this done on the sly. You don't want the police showing up, do you?"

"She has a point," I said and looked at my ring. Spencer wouldn't take kindly to me breaking and entering and searching for dead bodies in a coffee shop. "We should try to be quiet."

"You mean I stole this jackhammer from their contractor for nothing?" Ruth said. "No way. Do you know what it takes to steal a jackhammer without getting caught? It weighs more than me. I had to sneak it away from Urijah while his back was turned. I pulled three discs in my back, and I'm pretty sure my belly button is no longer in the same place, if you know what I mean."

I had no idea what she meant. "Urijah is the contractor for Buckstars?" I asked. The whole thing was becoming incestuous. The Essexes were swinging with God knew who, Ford had done business with Brad, who had met with Urijah, who was Ford and Liz's contractor. And by the way, also Spencer's contractor, which meant that he was my contractor. What the hell was going on?

"We need to get under that floor," I said. It was my only lead to solve the murder and save Bridget from having her baby in jail.

"That's what I want to hear. Grab the jackhammer," Ruth ordered Lucy.

"Hold the phone. What's that?" she asked, pointing. I froze.

"What? Have we been found out?" I asked, looking around with my night vision goggles.

"No," Lucy said, sounding annoyed. "What's that on your hand?"

"Oh, this."

"It's an engagement ring, of course," Ruth said. "What do you think it is? Spencer and Gladie are getting married."

"Wait a second. Wait a second," Lucy said, putting her arms out, as if she was walking the high wire without a net. "You told Ruth that you got engaged, but you didn't tell me?"

"She sort of guessed. I was going to tell you, but then all of this happened, and Bridget's in trouble."

Lucy looked ashen, even through the lens of the night vision goggles. I had broken the best friend code. I should have called her the first moment that Spencer showed me the ring.

"It just happened," I said. "Last night."

"Twenty-four hours?"

"Twenty-five, tops," I said. "Can you forgive me?"

A smile grew on her face, slowly. "You're getting married to Spencer! True love has conquered the day! I knew it would happen!"

"The cop is finally settling down," Uncle Harry said, lighting up a cigar. "It's like you tagged Bigfoot. Congratulations, Legs. When's the wedding?"

"The wedding?" I asked. I hadn't actually thought of the wedding. I didn't want to be the center of attention and walk down the aisle with Wagner playing.

"Can we focus, people?" Ruth asked. "We have a dead body to dig up. You can figure out bridesmaids' dresses at another time."

"Bridesmaids' dresses, Gladie. You hear that?" Lucy asked.

Oh, God. Bridesmaids' dresses. What had I done?

"We're standing around like morons in night vision goggles. We have to be serious. There's a dead body to dig up before the swingers come back from their orgy party."

"Who's a swinger at an orgy party?" Lucy asked.

"The Buckstars owners," I explained. "They're swingers."

Lucy slammed her hand down on a table. "There are swingers in this little town? Nobody ever tells me anything!"

"Tick, tock," Ruth said. "Are we doing this or what?"

We were doing it. Ruth agreed to leave her stolen jackhammer behind because it would be too noisy. Uncle Harry had brought two of his "assistants" with him, plus a couple shovels. Along with the jackhammer, Ruth had stolen the alarm key, and she pushed the code into the keypad. Our criminal group walked inside. It was already a miracle that we hadn't been spotted by someone, but thankfully, the town was either boiling eggs or bonking strangers.

"This is going to be hard without a jackhammer," Ruth grumbled.

"I told you that I brought muscle," Harry insisted, and he signaled to his two men, who put their shovels aside and pulled out guns from their jackets.

"What the hell?" I said.

They shot a flurry of bullets into the floor. The tile went flying. When they were done, I slapped my hands on my ears, which were ringing. "That's not quieter than a jackhammer!" Ruth yelled. The guns were loud enough to wake the dead. We froze and waited for the police to come.

But nobody came. It was a miracle.

"All right. Start digging," Harry ordered his men.

"I can't believe they shot up the floor," Ruth grumbled. "And you guys acted like I was stupid for stealing a jackhammer."

The two men made quick work of the floor. They ripped up every inch of the store, trying to find a dead person. Buckstars looked like it had been bombed. There was tile and dirt everywhere. The tables and chairs were piled high in the corner. We had to stand at the doorway in order not to fall into the deep holes. The men dug down six feet before we found something.

"What is it?" Ruth asked.

"It's a body part," Lucy said. "Maybe an arm?'

"That ain't no arm," Harry said.

"It's not a body," I said. "I don't even think that's human."

One of Uncle Harry's men picked it up and raised it over his head. "It's a dildo. They killed a dildo!"

"They buried a dildo?" Ruth said. "What kind of sick people are they?"

Since we were standing in what looked a battlefield in World War One, I didn't feel right talking about the sickness of other people.

"Holy crap," Lucy breathed. "They really are swingers."

"Where's the body? There was supposed to be a body," I said.

"We could bust through the walls," one of Uncle Harry's men suggested. "Walls are good for hiding bodies."

"What have we done?" I asked, taking stock of the rubble that once was Buckstars.

"Right?" Ruth said. "This is better than flooding the bathrooms. What should we do with the dildo? I have some Superglue. We could stick it to the front door."

"I'm a bad person," I breathed. "I've destroyed a business." I had turned into a criminal, all because I didn't want Bridget to be accused of being a criminal. I had gone over to the dark side. "I can't even afford to make it right. I'm not an expert, but I bet that a new floor costs more than twenty-seven bucks and a five-dollar gift card to Barnes & Noble."

"Who gave you a gift card to Barnes & Noble?" Lucy asked me.

"Okay, fine. Just twenty-seven bucks."

"I don't know what's eating you, Gladie," Ruth said. "I've

never felt happier. I've got cocaine-level endorphins running through me. These Buckstars people are bad."

I had been hoping that they were murderers. Burying a dildo was not on the same level as murder. "I'm a criminal. I'm a vandal."

Uncle Harry put his arm around my shoulders. "You're just in a slump. Normally, you peg the killer right off. This time you were off a little. Everyone hits a rough patch. Would it make you feel better if I leave some cash for the dildo people? Enough so that they can rebuild or buy more dildos, whichever they prefer?"

"Would you?"

"Sure."

I was relieved that the Essexes would be reimbursed for our vandalism, but I was worried that Harry was right about my slump. I wasn't any closer to solving the mystery of Brad's murder, and now I wasn't sure I would ever prove Bridget's innocence.

CHAPTER 13

Nothing good happens after midnight. If your matches aren't home in bed by then, they're only asking for trouble. You ever hear of Cinderella? That was just the tip of the iceberg, dolly.

Lesson 104, Matchmaking advice from your Grandma Zelda

I slept the sleep of the deeply ashamed, which ironically meant that I slept like a rock. I didn't even hear Spencer when he came to bed in the middle of the night. It was the kind of sleep without dreams, which was out of the ordinary for me.

A little before six in the morning, I woke up with a start when the doorbell rang. Spencer was still asleep next to me, snoring up a storm. Who could be at the door before six? I thought back to the shootout at Buckstars and was sure that the cops had come to get me. But not the regular cops.

The vandalism cops.

"Oh, my God. The vandalism cops are after me," I whispered.

I didn't want to go to jail. The doorbell rang, again. Spencer stirred. It wouldn't be good for me if Spencer knew the vandalism cops were after me. It also wouldn't be good to wake my grandmother, because she was still recovering and needed her sleep. I hopped out of bed and put on a pair of sweats.

After closing the door to my bedroom, I took the stairs two and a time and answered the door. The entire Easter egg hunt committee was there. They pushed past me and stormed into the parlor.

"It's a disaster," Josephine complained, throwing her hands up. It was the first time I had seen her without makeup. Her hair was frizzy and tied back in a ponytail. She looked like she hadn't slept.

"I've boiled fifteen thousand eggs," Griffin moaned. He was wearing pajama bottoms and a UCLA sweatshirt. "All for nothing."

"The horror! The horror!" the mayor bellowed. Normally dapper and well-dressed, he was wearing the same thing I was, sweats and a t-shirt. The whole committee looked like they had been pulled out of their beds. The only one wearing real clothes was the world record man, who had on a suit with a half-buttoned shirt, no tie, and his briefcase clutched to his chest, as if he was worried that someone was going to steal it. He had the unmistakable look of a visitor thrust into the bizarro world of Cannes.

"What's going on?" I whispered to Alice.

"It looks like the hunt is being called off on account of murderers and drug dealers."

"Oh, good," I said. "What a relief. Wait a minute. What do you mean?"

The doorbell rang, interrupting her. I stuck a finger in the air. "I'll be right back," I told Alice and went for the door.

This time it was Bridget. Her belly looked bigger.

"I need pickled," she said and walked past me.

"Pickled? You mean pickles?"

I followed her into the kitchen, where she opened the refrigerator. "I mean pickled. Everything pickled. And your grandmother is the only one I know who has pickled everything."

She was right. There was an entire pickled shelf in the fridge. Pickled cucumbers, pickled beets, pickled turnips. All kinds of pickled. Bridget put the jars on the table, and I handed her a plate.

She popped a pickled turnip in her mouth and shut her eyes in appreciation. "I couldn't sleep all night. My cravings were so strong. I walked around the town but nothing helped," she said with her mouth full.

"Are you feeling all right? How's the baby?"

"Fine. My tax season is over, thank goodness. Lucy told me that you had a lead on Brad's murder."

A wave of hope washed over Bridget's face. "It was sort of a dead end," I told her. The hope vanished from her face, and she put a forkful of pickled beet in her mouth.

"I was hoping something was moving because of the ruckus last night," she said.

"You mean the gunshots?"

"There were gunshots?"

"You know, into the floor tile."

"What floor tile?"

"Hold on," I said. "What are you talking about? What ruckus? You mean, Buckstars?"

She pointed at me and nodded. Her cheeks were distended, like a chipmunk, full of pickled vegetables. "Buckstars. That's it. Those Buckstars people. Didn't Spencer tell you about the raid and the FBI?"

My mind raced with possibilities for an FBI raid. I worried that Lucy and Ruth got caught up in it. "Spencer got home when I was asleep. What happened?"

"I saw the FBI drive into town. There was a sting at the Buckstars' owners' house. Drugs."

My brain tried to make sense of it all. The committee wanted to call off the Easter egg hunt because of murder and drugs. And maybe the two went together. Ford Essex had been in business with Brad. Was it the drugs business? If Ford was a drug smuggler with Brad, it all made sense, and it made Ford the obvious murder suspect.

"This means you're off the hook," I told Bridget, excited. "Now Ford will be the number one suspect."

"Really?"

My phone rang. "Gladie? Gladie Burger? This is Bruce. Oh, Gladie!"

It was the match I had made for Terri. "Bruce, it's six in the morning." The only time a match had ever called my grandmother at six in the morning was because of a Viagra malfunction.

"I'm at the hospital," he said.

"Bruce, you're only supposed to take one pill at a time."

"What? I didn't take any pills. I'm here with Terri. Oh, Gladie, it was terrible!"

"She's in the hospital?"

"Yes," Bruce said. "I had to sign a waiver because she's not capable."

"Gallbladder?" I asked.

"No."

"Kidney stones?"

"No."

"Appendix?"

"No."

"What are we talking about here, Bruce? Are we talking lockjaw level or Ebola level?"

"So much worse, Gladie. So much worse."

"Aliens!" I heard a woman shout on the other end of the phone. "Beam me up, Scotty, can bite me on the ass. Where's my gun? I need to shoot me some aliens!"

"What do I do, Gladie?" Bruce asked.

Griffin walked into the kitchen and gave Bridget the stink eye. "This is your fault!" he yelled at her. "You've ruined the egg hunt! I'm going to sue you! Why aren't you in jail?"

Bridget started to cry and spit a mouthful of half-chewed pickled vegetables onto the table.

"Bruce, can I call you back?" I asked into the phone.

"No! I need help now. You did this! You're responsible for this!"

"Okay. Okay. I'll meet you at the hospital in thirty minutes."

"All right," Bruce said. "I don't think she can bite through the restraints in thirty minutes."

I hung up the phone and stood up. Wow, matchmaking was not as easy as it was portrayed on TV.

"Griffin, don't talk to Bridget that way," I ordered and pointed to her stomach. "She's pregnant."

"Spawn of the devil," Griffin said. "Everyone knows she killed that guy, and now the egg hunt is canceled."

A few committee members came into the kitchen. "I beg to differ. I beg to differ," the mayor said, wagging his finger. "Not about Bridget killing that poor, unfortunate man. I differ about the Easter egg hunt. The hunt isn't canceled. We will prevail and overcome our now tarnished reputation as a sex-crazed, drug fiend, murder town."

"With an Easter egg hunt," Josephine said, not sounding convinced.

"World record Easter egg hunt," the mayor corrected. "We're not going to let the little ones down. This is a service we're doing."

"What if she kills again?" Griffin demanded. I was getting furious at him for attacking my best friend.

Bridget slammed her hand on the table. "I didn't kill Brad!" she shouted, like she was in a scene from *The Exorcist.* "I'm an unflinching, never tiring advocate of human rights. Unflinching, never tiring advocates of human rights don't stab men to death!"

"Likely story!" Griffin shouted back.

Bridget poked him in the chest as she spoke. "I'm going to sue you for slander! Slander! Or worse!" she yelled and poked him repeatedly, like she had gotten hold of Ruth's jackhammer and was digging for dildos.

"Ow!" Griffin yelled and jumped backward, slapping his hand over his chest, as if he had been shot. "Did you all see that? The murderess attacked me and threatened me! Did you see that?"

"I did not! I would never attack a human being!" Bridget yelled and threw a handful of pickled turnips at his head. They landed with a splat, and the committee members gasped in unison.

"If you weren't pregnant, I would punch you in the face!" Griffin yelled.

"If you weren't a creep, I would...I would...I don't know!" Bridget yelled back and threw another handful of pickled turnips at him. She wasn't good at being mean. I put my arm around her.

"Come on, Bridget. Let's get out of here."

"You're lucky I wasn't craving bone-in beef ribs!" she yelled at Griffin and walked out with me.

We left the house and stood outside by my grandmother's rosebushes. "It'll work out," I said. "The weird Essex people are now the number one suspects." But I didn't know that for sure. All I knew was that they had buried a dildo in their coffee shop. But probably that was one step away from murder.

"What's that?" she asked, looking down.

"What?"

"Your finger. There's something on your finger. Did Spencer put that on your finger?" She sniffed and wiped her nose on the back of her hand. "And it's a sapphire, so you didn't get a blood diamond, which is responsible." She began to blubber. "I love love. I love my baby even though he's not born yet and even though the sperm that made him came from a monster."

"You're a very loving person, Bridget. Maybe you should get some rest."

"I'm so happy for you," she cried, giving me a hug. "Normally I don't approve of marriage, but Spencer is a good man. You know, even though he arrested me."

"I'm sorry about that."

"Do you smell that?" she asked.

"Sorry about that, too. I haven't showered, yet, and I was around a used dildo last night."

"Not that," Bridget said, looking around. "I smell eggs Benedict."

I didn't smell eggs Benedict, but my stomach growled just thinking about it. "Are you all right to be alone? I have to go to the hospital. You could come with me. I would like your company."

"Maybe later. I think I'm going to go for a walk and get some fresh air and find the eggs. Then, I'm going to grab a quick nap or eat a cheesecake. Lunch?"

I kissed her on the cheek. "Lunch," I agreed.

I went back inside. The committee had moved to the entranceway, and Alice had pinned Griffin on the floor. Wow, she sure was strong.

"Cool it, pal, or I'll choke you out!" she warned him.

"Can't we all be friends?" the mayor asked. His world record representative was clutching his briefcase tighter to his chest.

"Shut up," Josephine growled. "You're dumber than a Victoria's Secret model without her wings."

"Now, that's uncalled for, Josephine," the mayor said. "Listen, committee members. We're so close to painting those eggs. We can make this happen!"

"Let me up! I'm outta here," Griffin said. Alice let him up, and he stormed out of the house.

Spencer stumbled down the stairs, rubbing his tired eyes. "Are you kidding me? What's going on here?"

"Committee members," the mayor said, ignoring Spencer. "We must remain strong. We can make this happen. We can show the world that Cannes is worthy. So, disperse to your kitchens. Finish boiling those eggs and start painting!"

There was a murmuring and a couple outbursts of "we can do it." I decided to push them over the edge in order to get rid of them so that I could go to the hospital and check on my match.

"You can do it! You'll beat the record!" I yelled with my hand up, like I was the Statue of Liberty. It worked. Filled with renewed enthusiasm, they left to boil more eggs. Phew. I couldn't wait until the Easter egg hunt was finished.

Spencer ran his hand over his hair and hugged me. "Am I wrong, or are these matchmaking meetings getting earlier and more violent?"

"It was an egg meeting."

"This is such a crazy town," Spencer said. "Last night the feds came in to quash a drug smuggling operation, and you'll never guess who the drug smugglers were."

"I have no idea," I lied.

"Those Buckstars people. And the topper was that they

were sex maniacs, too. Not that I have anything against sex maniacs, but these guys were off the charts. We busted in when they were having a sex party. Old people getting it on for as far as the eye could see."

"Gross," I said, not letting Spencer know that we were almost participants in the sex party.

"And that's not the craziest part," he added.

"There's a crazier part than the drug smuggling sex party?" I asked.

"Yes. For some reason, those lunatics also dug up the entire floor of their new coffee place and Superglued dildos all over the front door."

"More than one dildo?" I asked.

"At least a dozen. Now, if you want to push or pull the door to Buckstars, you've got a hand full of shlong."

"Bizarre," I said, wondering how Ruth got her hands on a dozen dildos. But I didn't like where the conversation was going, which was too close to Spencer finding out that I was responsible for the Buckstars vandalism. "Oh no, I have to go. Matchmaking emergency," I said, pulling away from him.

"That's fine. I have to get to work. Terri called in sick. I hope she isn't faking."

I nodded. "That would suck."

After getting my purse, I ran outside and opened my car door. I was shocked to see Griffin sitting on the passenger seat, his face against the window. Seeing him there, hiding with only the back of his head in view, he looked like a man, dejected. Like a man who had boiled fifteen thousand eggs and had gotten pulverized with pickled turnips by a pregnant woman.

I sat down and put my seatbelt on. "Hiding out, huh?" I asked him. "It's been a tough few days, for sure. Would you mind if I drove to the hospital? I have a matchmaking emergency. You can come along, if you want."

He didn't answer, so I took his silence for a yes. I turned the motor on and backed out of the driveway. "Beautiful day," I said. There was a huge crowd on Main Street in front of Buckstars. Ruth was standing on the sidewalk, looking at her handiwork with a big smile on her face. She waved as I drove by, and I waved back.

"I think this murder thing is going to get wrapped up, quickly, Griffin," I continued. "By the time you get the world record for biggest Easter egg hunt, Ford Essex will be behind bars, and not just behind bars for drug smuggling. I have it on good authority that he had been in the drug business with Brad. So, you see, Bridget had nothing to do with it."

I rubbed his arm for a second. "I'm so sad to see you so low, Griffin. I know you've been under a lot of stress. Don't you worry about it. Take the time you need to recover." I turned into the hospital's parking lot and parked by the entrance. "You want to come in with me or stay in the car?" He didn't answer and slumped further against his window. "I get it. You need more time."

I cracked my window and left Griffin in the car. I had no idea what I was walking into. Bruce had said the date had gone bad, but that could have meant a million things from bad breath to an armed brother to typhoid. I hoped it wasn't typhoid because I wasn't good around communicable diseases.

I called Bruce when I walked into the lobby. "Where are you?"

"Emergency Room. Third bed on the right."

I knew the Emergency Room well. I had gone there when I had stepped on a nail. Business was booming today, but I found Terri's bed quickly. I gasped when I saw her.

"Yep, they bandaged her entire face," Bruce said, at her bedside. "I have no idea what's going on underneath. She started off looking like Gisele, but now, it's anybody's guess." He shook his head, like he was sorry his football team was having a rotten season.

"What happened?" I asked. I didn't want to know, but as the matchmaker, I was responsible.

"It was going great," Bruce explained. "I brought her the kitten, and she loved it. Golly, Terri was so pretty. Like a doll. I almost asked her to marry me right then and there."

"Did she like you, too?" If Fred was her type, then Bruce would probably be her type, too, but there was no accounting for taste.

"I think so. I asked her to get a bite to eat with me, and she said yes."

"That's great!" I cheered, giving him a quick hug. Matchmaking was very satisfying when it worked.

"It was great," he agreed, running his hand over his hair. "She changed into a pretty outfit, and she put on makeup and lots of perfume. She smelled great," he said and sighed, deeply. I wanted to tell him that I had given her the perfume, but I was impatient to hear the rest of the story. "We went to a little place I know, and she told me all about her family and about how she used to be a detective, but some nosy woman cost her her job."

"That part's not too interesting," I said. "Then what happened?

"It was going real well. We had chemistry. So, we went back to my place."

"Already? Not that I'm judging."

Bruce's face turned a light shade of red. "Like I said, the chemistry was real good."

I nodded. "I've been there. Go on."

"I got five cats, you know. There's Milly and Geronimo and Blackie and…"

"I don't need to know about the cats, Bruce. What happened to Terri?"

"Aliens!" Terri shouted from her bed. "Aliens did this to me!"

The nurse ran to her bed and injected something into Terri's IV. "We keep upping the dose, but she's got the constitution of a horse," the nurse said.

"Aliens did this to her?" I asked Bruce.

"No. Petunia did."

"Petunia?"

Bruce put his hand up, as if he was testifying to Congress. "As God is my witness, I forgot about Petunia's aversion."

"Who's Petunia?"

"My cat. Normally, she's a sweet little tabby. Cute as a button. She loves to play with my mouse on a stick. Such a cutie pie."

"The cutie pie did this to Terri's face?" I asked.

Bruce put his hand on his face and dropped his head to his chest. "I forgot about the perfume. Petunia hates perfume. She doesn't mind deodorant or a spritz or two of scent, but she can't handle real strong perfume."

I didn't like where this was going.

"The minute Terri walked into the place, it was Apocalypse Now," Bruce said, looking into space, like he was reliving a bad dream. "I've never seen anything like it. Petunia first screeched. It was a sound I had never heard before. Nothing like it in nature, Gladie. Nothing."

I patted him on his back. "There. There. I'm sorry you're traumatized."

"Thank you. I'll never stop seeing my little tabby Petunia spring into the air. She looked like one of those flying squirrels in the Amazon, but she was going up instead of down. Her legs were stretched long to the sides, and her claws were out and eerily long."

"Like Wolverine," I breathed, envisioning the horror of Petunia.

Bruce pointed at me. "That's it. That's it exactly. Petunia was just like Wolverine. She opened her mouth, hell bent on clawing Terri's face and erasing the smell of her fancy perfume." Bruce bit down on his knuckle and suppressed a cry.

"Then, what happened?" I urged.

"It was awful. Petunia leaped onto Terri's face, like it was Alien versus Predator. At first, Terri didn't realize what was going on. It was like she thought Petunia was playing with her. Then, when Petunia bit down on the top of Terri's head, she knew. Oh, Lord, she knew! Petunia was screaming. Terri was screaming. I was screaming. There was a whole lot of screaming, Gladie! Terri spun around and tried to rip Petunia off her face, but Petunia was locked in good with her long claws. Terri spun around and knocked into the television, making it fall to the floor. Then, she spun around again and knocked into the recliner and then the kitchen counter and then the knife set. I stood there frozen. I couldn't move a muscle. Maybe because I couldn't believe what I was seeing."

Bruce took a deep breath, and we both looked at Terri. She was drugged to the gills, but she moved her head from side to side, as if she was still locked in battle with Petunia.

"It lasted forever," Bruce continued. "Until I finally came to and offered Petunia a bowl of Half-n-Half. That's her favorite, you know."

"I like Half-n-Half, too," I said.

Bruce nodded. "I filled up her saucer, and Petunia jumped off of Terri's face like she was happy as a clam and went for the cream. That's when Terri fainted, and I got a good look at her." He shuddered and covered his eyes with his hand. "Oh, Gladie. Terri didn't look like Gisele, anymore."

"What did she look like?"

"She looked like my grandmother's meatloaf."

"This isn't your fault, Bruce," I said, truthfully. Fear crawled up my spine. Terri was going to kill me when they took the IV out. "Does Terri know that I set you two up?"

"No, ma'am. I kept that under my hat, just like we discussed."

"You might want to keep that a secret forever," I said. It was bad enough that she was going to kill me for giving her the perfume. I didn't want to take any more blame than that. "Anyway, I'm sure they can fix her up," I said. "Modern medicine is miraculous."

"I don't care," Bruce said, taking Terri's hand in his. "I love her. I want her to be my bride. I don't care if she looks like my grandmother's meatloaf. Do you think she'll forgive me about Petunia?"

From my experience, Terri wasn't the forgiving type. But chemistry was chemistry, so it was possible Terri would forgive him. "Maybe you can keep Petunia under your hat, too. Blame it on the aliens."

Bruce's face brightened with hope. "That's a genius idea, Gladie. Aliens!"

"Aliens," Terri moaned.

It was probably not a good thing to base a relationship on lies, but since I had lied to Spencer at least five times in the past couple of days, who was I to judge? Besides, I had made a match and saved Fred. I also wasn't going to get any more tickets at least until Terri was discharged.

It was a good day.

I left the hospital and walked back to my car. There was a nasty smell in the parking lot. Griffin was still in the car where I left him. I got in and sat down. The smell was worse, and I opened my window all the way.

"Not feeling any better?" I asked Griffin. I started the motor and drove out of the parking lot. "Is there somewhere I can drop you off? Somebody you want to see? Maybe you just need some rest. Where do you live? You've been working so hard, lately. You probably need a day in bed. Would you like that? A day in bed?"

We went over a speed bump too fast, and I hit my head on the ceiling. Griffin took that moment to put his head in my lap.

"Whoa, buddy!" I yelled, and the car swerved. I tried to push Griffin away from my crotch, but he was big and wouldn't be moved. "When I said, bed, I didn't mean my bed. This isn't the way to make yourself feel better. I'm engaged. Didn't you see my ring? It's an engagement ring. I don't have the same feelings for you, Griffin!"

I got control of the car and pulled to the side of the road. "I mean, it Griffin! Get off me."

That when I saw the blood in my lap. And that's when I realized the bad smell was coming from Griffin, and it wasn't body odor or gas. "Griffin?" I asked and heaved him off of me.

That's when I saw more blood. Lots and lots of blood.

CHAPTER 14

Matches make themselves meshugi, trying to be perfect before they find love. So, they exercise. Exercise! What mamzer invented exercise? It used to be that we walked in order to get somewhere. Now, we're walking on a fakakta machine, walking, walking, walking and getting nowhere. What's the purpose of that, bubbeleh? Call me crazy, but a gap between your thighs doesn't sound like a reason to walk for miles without actually moving. So, tell your matches to relax. Sure, take a walk. But make it count. Get somewhere.

Lesson 5, Matchmaking advice from your Grandma Zelda

I slept until it was Friday and the stink of dead body was off of me. I was thankful for the sleep because being awake had sucked balls.

On Tuesday, when I had finally figured out that I had been driving around a corpse, I started to scream, and I didn't stop until my voice was gone.

"Let me get this straight," Spencer said to me in his office at the police station, after a passerby called the police and I had been brought in to see why I had a murdered person in my car. "You drove a stiff all around town."

"And I talked to him. I had a whole conversation with him," I told Spencer, my voice still hoarse.

It was quiet in the police station. After the big drug bust the night before, I was the only action in town. While I sat in Spencer's office, facing him across from his desk, with a lap full of Griffin's blood, the hallway was crammed with police loitering and straining to listen in.

"Did he talk back?" Spencer asked me.

I heard light giggling in the hallway.

"No. I rambled on and on, giving him advice on how to reduce his stress, and he just listened to me."

Spencer nodded. "I see."

"Is that odd? I mean, that's happened before, right?"

He scratched the side of his head. "What? A dead guy listening to you or driving a dead guy around town?"

"The second one."

"Nope. That's never happened."

I squinted at him and gave him my meanest look. "I'm reasonably sure it's happened. I remember hearing something about Julia Roberts and a dead guy in her Land Rover." I didn't know what I was saying. I had chunks of Griffin's face on my lap, and I wasn't feeling well.

"I must have missed the story about Julia Roberts. Didn't you notice that he wasn't breathing?"

"Excuse me if it didn't occur to me to check his breathing. Do you normally check my breathing?"

"I don't have to. You never stop talking."

I gasped. "Why are you being mean to me right now? I have dead person on me. Oh my God. My car. My car has dead person in it. How am I going to get that out of the leather? And poor Griffin. You don't care about Griffin."

"I care about Griffin. A man was murdered in my town."

No lie, he was sounding like John Wayne, and I was getting turned on. I looked at my ring. Somehow it had escaped the blood and gore. But it wasn't the moment to think about Spencer's sexiness or my jewelry.

"Was Griffin stabbed like Brad was?" I asked.

"Looks that way."

"I think the Essex couple are your main suspects," I said.

"I'm pretty sure that Brad was Ford's partner in his drug business, and Liz told me that there was a body buried in Buckstars."

"Griffin Rose was murdered at around six-thirty this morning. The Essexes have been in a federal holding cell about two miles away since 2:00 AM."

"Oh."

"Interesting about the dead body, though, considering their whole shop was dug up."

"Yeah, interesting," I muttered. "You know Alice is strong, and she mentioned that if she killed someone, she would..."

"Let me stop you right there, Miss Marple," Spencer interrupted. "We've arrested Bridget."

I stood up. "You what?" I screeched. "She had nothing to do with this. She was looking for eggs Benedict when this happened."

But I wasn't sure of that. I had left Bridget in the front yard when I went back into the house. It was possible that she was still there when Griffin had stormed out. But there was no way Bridget could have murdered him or anyone else. Murder was not in her makeup. It would have been impossible.

"Poor Bridget," I said. "She's pregnant, you know. You can't let her rot in jail."

Spencer shook his head. "We're giving her a monitoring

bracelet, and she's moving in with Lucy and Harry for the time being."

That was a relief. At least she would be taken care of. "I need to help her," I said.

"You need to go home and rest."

"And Grandma. I need to help Grandma," I said.

"She's home with Meryl. Last I saw, they were watching an old movie on my television and eating fried chicken for breakfast."

At the mention of fried chicken, my stomach roiled. "I think I'm going to be sick," I said.

And I was. I threw up three times and made a mess out of the women's bathroom in the police station. With my statement complete, Spencer drove me home. He was keeping my car as evidence. After checking on my grandmother, I took a long shower and went to bed. I didn't get up until Friday morning, totally skipping Wednesday and Thursday.

"Fred? Is that you?" I asked when I finally woke. He was sitting in the chair next to my bed staring at me.

"Hey there, Underwear Girl. You took a mighty big nap. Gee, you look pretty when you sleep. And when you're awake, too. Even with the drool and your hair like that."

"Thank you. What are you doing here?"

"I'm on the seven-to-eleven shift. I'm guarding you."

"Guarding me from who?"

"The Chief doesn't know. It could be a lot of people. You have more than a few who want you dead, I guess. How do you feel?"

"Thirsty. Hungry."

"You want me to make breakfast? I know how to make French toast."

"Really? I wouldn't mind a slice of French toast." I swung my legs off the bed, and I got dizzy. "Or five. Who am I kidding? Just make the whole loaf, Fred."

"All right, Underwear Girl. Stay away from the windows, just in case."

I looked at the window. "Is Spencer worried that Griffin's killer is going to come after me?"

Fred shrugged. "I think he's more worried about Terri coming after you."

"Excuse me?"

"You want powdered sugar or maple syrup with your French toast?" he asked, leaving my room.

"Yes," I said.

I was worried about his Terri comment, but sweet, fried bread was my priority after not eating for more than twenty-four hours. I went to the bathroom and peed a gallon and dressed in jeans and a cotton sweater.

Slipping a pair of Spencer's socks on my feet, I padded down the hall to my grandmother's room, but she wasn't there. I walked downstairs and found her in the kitchen with Fred.

"Hi, Dolly. There's coffee in the pot. Fred's making us French toast. Isn't that nice?"

"More than nice. Hey Fred, what did you mean about Terri? Is she out of the hospital?"

"She escaped yesterday," my grandmother answered, putting her hand on mine.

"She's got cat scratch fever," Fred explained, cracking eggs into a bowl.

"What do they do for that? Tylenol?" I asked.

Fred seemed to think about that for a minute. "I don't know if they tried that."

"She needs more than Tylenol," Grandma explained. "She's got a dose of crazy. It's going to last a few more days."

She was already more than slightly crazy. I wouldn't want to cross her when she was even crazier.

Fred dipped bread into the egg mixture. "The Chief has half of the patrolmen out looking for her. There was a Terri sighting at the pharmacy yesterday. She was looking for an aliens vaccine. But the last sighting had her saying she was going to get 'Stinking Gladie.' I don't know what she's talking about. I think you smell real nice, Underwear Girl."

I wasn't happy to hear that Terri was after me. She had already been after me, but that was before she was scratched by a cat and turned into some kind of crazed supervillain. Who knew cats had such power?

Fred dropped the bread into a pan, and it sizzled. My stomach growled. I got up and poured myself a cup of coffee and added some milk.

"How are you feeling, Grandma?" I asked, taking a sip of the coffee and sitting back down next to her.

"I'm feeling more and more like myself. Uh oh. The mayor's here."

"Huh?" I asked, just as I heard the front door open.

"Hello, there! Anyone home?" the mayor called and then laughed at his joke because my grandmother never left her property line. He walked into the kitchen. "Hello, townspeople," he gushed. "I have big news. Big! You don't mind if I help myself to some coffee, do you, Zelda?"

"Go ahead. The pot's fresh."

He poured himself a cup. "Fred, are you making a couple of slices for me?"

"No, sir."

The mayor laughed and slapped Fred on his back. "Good one, Fred! Good one! Just give me a plate when it's done." He sat down across from me. "Wonderful egg news. Our Easter egg hunt is going as planned. All boiled and accounted for."

"Really? All five hundred and one thousand?" I asked, surprised that I was actually excited that the town had managed to boil all of the eggs for the world record.

"Yes, miss. We've moved on to the painting phase of the process. Mr. Jones from Paramount World Records is very impressed with our little town, I have to tell you. This is going to put us on the map!"

My grandmother smiled at me, and I blushed. My first official town decision had worked. Sure, the co-chair had been murdered, but otherwise, it was going without a hitch. I had almost replaced Zelda Burger. I was a success. Sort of.

"What's your news?" Grandma asked him.

"We got a big celebrity for Sunday. Guess where he's flying in from?"

"Alcatraz?" I asked.

"No. England. A celebrity from England! We were very lucky to have him. It's a good thing you voted for a mayor who had international contacts. Just think of it! A celebrity from England coming here for our Easter egg hunt."

Fred served the French toast, and we dug in. "Delicious, Fred. Thank you," I told him.

"I'll tell you this is the biggest event this town has ever seen since Barbra Streisand's second cousin judged the apple pie eating contest back in seventy-seven," the mayor said with his mouth full of French toast. "Now, Gladie, can you tell me if you're going to find any more dead people before the event or, heaven forbid, the day of the event?"

Everyone looked at me. "It doesn't work that way," I said. "I mean, I don't know ahead of time."

The mayor's face dropped. "Oh, I thought you were like your grandmother."

Grandma shrugged. "Gladie's got the gift."

"I don't know who's going to die or when, but I do know that Bridget is innocent," I said. "She didn't kill Brad, and she didn't kill Griffin."

"That's good because she does my books, and I don't want anyone else to know how much I spend on satin sheets and laser hair removal," the mayor said.

The four of us chewed our French toast. I was happy that the mayor believed me about Bridget's innocence. Pouring more syrup on my plate, I realized that I knew Bridget was innocent, and it wasn't just because she was my best friend and I wanted her to be innocent. Somehow, I was absolutely certain that she wasn't the killer. Unfortunately, I had no idea who actually was the killer, however. Perhaps my Miss Marple really was broken inside me.

"So, Griffin didn't give you any hints before he died?" Fred asked.

"He was already dead, so our conversation was one-sided."

Conversation. Conversation. The word tickled my brain, waking a memory, but I couldn't remember which memory. Conversation. Conversation with Griffin. Griffin talking. Griffin killed. Griffin stabbed to death. Conversation.

Hmmm...

I used my last piece of French toast to sop up the maple syrup. Then it hit me. "Holy shit!" I shouted, jumping up from my seat. "Griffin was the voice!"

It came to me like a bolt out of the blue. Griffin's voice was the voice I heard in Buckstars about murder. Griffin must have killed Brad. But who killed Griffin?

"You all right there, Gladie?" the mayor asked.

"Maybe she has cat scratch fever, too," Fred suggested.

"I'm getting closer to solving this thing," I said to no one in particular. "It's a town-wide conspiracy. Everyone's involved, or almost everyone. I have to get to work. Will you be all right here, Grandma?"

"I'm fine, bubbeleh. I have to finish that fakakta needlepoint."

"Don't forget that I'm guarding you, Underwear Girl," Fred said.

"Good. We'll use your car. My car has chunks of brains in it."

"Drive faster," I ordered Fred.

"It's a thirty-mile-an-hour zone. Safety is a police officer's top concern."

"Step on it! Lives are on the line!"

Fred's mouth dropped open. "Yes, ma'am!" He revved the engine until we were going forty in the thirty-mile-an-hour zone. "Holy cow, I'm going to save lives. Am I going to shoot someone, too? 'Cause I probably should warn you that I'm not great on the firing range. Not that I'm allowed to go there anymore, after the incident."

"You probably won't have to shoot. Just wave your gun around like you're going to shoot."

"Awesome idea, Underwear Girl. Normally, pretty girls like you aren't smart, too. Have you had plastic surgery? Is that your real nose?"

We passed Buckstars, which was closed. There was police tape on the front door, weaved between the dozen dildos.

"We tried to get those off, but Superglue is a good product," Fred said. Next door, a steady stream of customers were going in and out of Tea Time. Not only had her competition disappeared, but now her customers got to gawk at the dildos on their way for a pot of tea. Ruth was a retail genius.

"Here!" I shouted, pointing at a small house. "Park here!"

Fred slammed on the brakes. I opened my door and hopped out. "Hold on, I have to protect you," he ordered. I ignored him and stomped up the steps and pounded on the door like it was a police raid.

"Keep your pants on!" I heard from inside the house.

Josephine opened the door. Her hair was back to normal, but her hands were blue. "Have you come to help with these damned eggs?"

She turned and walked into the house, and Fred and I followed her. Her kitchen had turned into an egg dyeing factory. She had stacks and stacks of egg crates, filled with blue eggs, and she had pots filled with dye.

"Wow, your hands sure are blue," I said.

"I'm dyeing eggs blue. What did you expect?"

"Oh, I don't know anything about Easter eggs. I thought you would wear gloves."

She seemed to think about that for a second, and she

pursed her lips. "Now you tell me! Someone could have told me that before I painted thousands of eggs. Gloves!" she yelled, slapping her forehead and leaving a blue handprint there. "Is this why you came here? To make fun of my hands?"

"No. I came to say that I know that you're in on it," I said.

"On what?"

"You know. Griffin. Ford. Liz. Brad. You're a drug smuggler, just like them."

She put her hands on her hips, leaving blue splotches on her shirt. "How dare you."

Fred took his gun out its holster and waved it at Josephine. "Not now, Fred," I whispered.

"Sorry," he said, holstering it, again.

"You're all in on it," I continued. "This town seems to attract drug dealers."

"I was born here. I've never touched drugs in my life."

"So you say!" I yelled at her, pointing my finger in her face. "But you were co-chairs with Griffin. You said you had seen a murdered body, and Alice said she would kill someone by stabbing them, and Urijah met with Brad. Griffin killed Brad and Urijah's goat and..." I drifted off. Nothing was sounding right. "And oh my God."

My brain was making calculations, like the Watson

computer on Jeopardy. Nothing was making sense. Nothing was the way it seemed.

Everyone was lying.

"You're not a drug smuggler?" I asked, knowing now that she wasn't.

Fred took his gun out again. "Spill the beans, or I'll drill you full of holes!"

"Not now, Fred," I whispered again.

"I'm not a drug smuggler, and I'd bet my house that Griffin wasn't either," she said. "He sold toilet brushes, for goodness sake. How dare you come in here and threaten me?"

"I'm sorry," I said, dejected. "I was just trying to help."

"Hogwash. I know who you are, Gladie Burger. You're always sticking your nose where it doesn't belong."

She was right. She was totally right. "That's not true," I said. "I just happen to find a lot of dead bodies."

"Maybe someone should look into you and what drugs you're sniffing. People dropping dead around you. Someone should investigate that!" She wasn't wrong. I was a death magnet. "And that poor cop woman. The whole town knows what you did to her. Now, she's wandering the streets like a lunatic. You did that to her."

"Have you seen her, lately?" Fred asked. "We've been

trying to catch her."

"Last I heard, she was in the laundromat, eating laundry detergent."

Yikes. Fred went outside to radio in Terri's location, and I did my best to apologize to Josephine.

"You have to understand that I've had a hard week," I began.

"You've had a hard week?" Josephine shrieked. "Have you prepared fifty thousand Easter eggs? Are you blue? I don't see any blue anywhere on you, you bitch."

Josephine quickly picked up a large pot full of blue dye and before I could flinch, she tossed it over my head.

"Now, you've had a hard week," she said, and pushed me toward the door.

I stood on the front porch and dripped blue dye. "Fred, my ring! My ring!" I called. He ran at me.

"You're blue," he said, stating the obvious.

"Save my ring. Take it and clean it off."

He pulled my ring off my finger and rubbed it on his uniform. "You look nice in blue," he said. "It matches your eyes."

"My eyes are green, Fred."

"Prettiest green in the world."

CHAPTER 15

Matches aren't always easy. They're not like hopping on the freeway to get to your destination. Sometimes you have to take the side roads and the dirt paths and sometimes, dolly, you have to go backward to go forward. It's hard to go backward when all you want to do is make your match. But things go wrong. Matches become impossible. Starting fresh is the only thing you can do to make the matches possible, again. So, don't be afraid to go backward. Go backward all the way to the beginning. But don't forget to watch where you're going bubbeleh, or you'll trip and land on your tuchus.

Lesson 130 Matchmaking advice from your Grandma Zelda

"I'm in love with a woman who's blue," Spencer said, smirking his little smirk. He was standing behind me in the bathroom, looking into the mirror. I was blue. We had tried everything to remove the dye from my skin, but nothing worked. I was so blue that I could have joined a show in Las Vegas.

"I thought it would have worn off by now. It's been over twenty-four hours." I had been hiding in the house since I had been blued by Josephine. My ring cleaned off beautifully, but I was all Smurf.

"At some point, you're going to have to leave the house, or are you going to become like Zelda?" he asked.

"You've enjoyed the housebound me." Spencer had taken up the guard duties from Fred, since under Fred's protection, I had turned blue. Spencer had made the most out of our time together. He bought a new television with all the bells and whistles, and when we weren't watching *Family Guy* in bed, he was working through his high school sexual fantasies during commercial breaks. With all of the sex, though, none of the blue rubbed off of me.

My grandmother was doing much better and was hosting Meryl's Saturday book club downstairs. "I really want one of Ruth's lattes, but I'm blue," I said, looking at my reflection.

"I'll take you."

He smiled, and I grew suspicious. "You seem awfully happy that I'm blue. You can't wait for the town to make fun of me."

"You haven't seen the town, lately. It's covered in eggs and dildos. I don't think they'll look twice at a blue woman."

For some reason, I believed him. Spencer and I walked to Tea Time. It was another gorgeous spring day in Cannes. "Grandma says that there's going to be a storm tomorrow, but there isn't a cloud in the sky," I said.

"Maybe she was talking about a metaphorical storm. I've got a crazy cop on the loose and twenty thousand children showing up tomorrow for the biggest Easter egg hunt in history. I think we're looking at a shit-storm brewing, Pinky."

Spencer was probably right. We turned onto Main Street. It was decked out in pastels and cardboard cutouts of Easter themes, like eggs and bunnies. I had to hand it to our town. It was crazy, but they sure knew how to volunteer.

"Careful," Spencer said, and pulled me out of the way of a pile of Easter eggs in the middle of the sidewalk. "They're everywhere, and they haven't finished hiding them," he explained.

I sidestepped another pile of eggs when Bruce Coyle ran by.

"Bruce!" I called, and he stopped. He squinted at me.

"Terri?" he asked.

"No, it's me. Gladie."

"You're blue."

"Really?" Spencer asked. "I hadn't noticed." He squinted at me, too. "Oh, look at that. Are you trying a new make-up,

Pinky?"

I punched him in the arm. "How are you, Bruce? Any word on Terri?"

Bruce shook his head. "There was a sighting in the Historic District about an hour ago. I was going to drive down here, but my truck was stolen. Good thinking, making yourself blue, Gladie. Maybe she won't recognize you this way."

I swallowed. So far, I had escaped the crazed revenge of Terri, but I didn't know how much longer my luck would hold. We said goodbye to Bruce, and Spencer and I walked into Tea Time.

"Latte, Ruth," I ordered.

"Sweet tea and a slice of pound cake," Spencer ordered.

We sat down at a center table. There were a dozen eggs in a basket in the middle of it. I looked around and noticed that Tea Time was practically stuffed to the rafters with eggs. It wasn't like Ruth to allow her beloved store to be used for town events, but perhaps she was feeling guilty for the dildos.

The shop had a few customers, about normal business for late afternoon on a Saturday. There were a few familiar faces, but just as Spencer had promised, they didn't give me a second look.

"What are we playing at today with the blue?" Ruth asked me coming to our table. "Is this some kind of millennial thing?"

"Yes," I answered.

"I saw that cop of yours today," Ruth told Spencer. "She was digging through my trash in the alley. You really need to be more careful in your hiring practices."

Spencer turned bright red. "Her online application was stellar," he said, even though he had worked with her in LA.

"That's the problem with this twenty-first century," Ruth complained. "Everything's online, and it's all crap. Nobody's face to face anymore. People are data. Data! You know what I care about data? Nothing, that's what. I wish I hadn't lived to see the twenty-first century. The twentieth century was bad enough. We're out of pound cake, but I have sour cream cake that will make you slap your mother. You want some of that?"

"Nobody sells cake better than you, Ruth," he said.

"Oh damn it," she said, looking at the door. "Here comes that moron mayor. Next time, let's vote for Urijah's goat."

"His goat was killed by aliens," I said.

Ruth grunted. "Damned twenty-first century."

The mayor walked in with the world record representative and a tall man who was dressed in an ill-fitting suit. "May I introduce you to Clovis Pemberley, our celebrity from England?" the mayor asked me. "Mr. Pemberley, this is Gladie Burger. Normally, she isn't blue."

"How do you do?" I asked.

"Just fine. This is my first trip to America. I'm very excited."

"Are you an actor?" I asked.

"Oh, no. I'm…" he began, but the mayor cut him off.

"Do we really need to know that?" the mayor said, tugging at his collar. "He's a celebrity, Gladie. A celebrity all the way from England. That's all we need to know."

Ruth came back with our drinks and the sour cream cake, and the mayor sat down with the mystery celebrity and the world record man. The door opened again, and Lucy floated in on a cloud of peach organza.

"There you are, darlin'. Damn it, you're blue. I was told that you were blue, but I didn't believe it. How crazy is that, that I missed you becoming blue? I miss everything. Is that sour cream cake? I love sour cream cake."

She stole Spencer's piece and took a bite, much to his chagrin.

"Where's Bridget? Is she all right?" I asked Lucy.

"She's home, writing her manifesto. She's been doing it nonstop for two days. There's a lot about the justice system and being wrongly accused in it, as you can imagine," she said, throwing Spencer a meaningful look.

"Don't look at me. I only work here," he said.

"Harry has his men watching the house, and I couldn't stand it one more minute," Lucy continued. "I said to myself, I'm not missing the action again. So, I'm sticking myself to you, Gladie. Whither you goest I will go, darlin."

"I don't think there's going to be any more action. It's just me and Spencer having coffee."

Lucy smiled and cocked her head to the side. "Look at you, two. You're like an old married couple. So cute together!" she gushed. Then, she leaned forward, and her expression grew serious. "Come on, what's happening with the murder mystery? Where are you in the investigation?"

"Oh, geez," Spencer groaned.

"I'm nowhere," I said.

"Because you're not law enforcement. Finally, you understand that. You're not Miss Marple," Spencer said.

"You take that back before I slap you," Lucy warned him.

"Nothing makes sense with these murders," I continued, ignoring Spencer. "The suspects seem to fit together, but they don't fit together. Everything is turned around and backward and upside down."

"Rats," Lucy said, taking another bite of the cake.

The door opened, and officer James walked in. "Chief,

we've got another aliens sighting, and it's a doozy," he told Spencer.

Spencer threw some bills down on the table. "Sorry, Pinky. I've got to take this. I've got to get these creeps. Damned frat boys gone wild, I'm sure."

He left Tea Time. "It's so weird about the aliens," Lucy told me. "They're going after brains. Stabbing this goat and that raccoon."

"What did you say?" I asked her.

"Aliens are going after brains."

"No. The other thing."

"They're stabbing goats and raccoons?"

I snapped my fingers. "That's it! That's it! That's where it all fits together. I've been looking at it backward and upside down because it's backward and upside down. Do you get it?"

Lucy knitted her eyebrows together. "No. Are we talking about the aliens?"

"I'm talking about everything. Is your car here?"

"Of course," she said. "You don't think I walked here in these heels, do you?"

I brought my latte with me into Lucy's peach Mercedes. "Where are we going?" Lucy asked as she started the car. "Is this going to be good? I have a pearl-handled gun in my purse in case I need to shoot somebody."

"I don't think we'll have to shoot anybody," I said. First Fred and now Lucy. Everyone wanted to shoot someone. "We're going back to the beginning of this stupid thing, where I should have started to begin with. I'm so stupid! I totally let my Miss Marple down."

"Oh, this is going to be good," Lucy sang cheerfully. "Holy crap, Gladie, look over there."

Terri was running down the street, wielding a cardboard cutout of a bunny over her head. She noticed me as we drove by, and she shook her fist at me and shouted something that I couldn't hear through the closed windows.

"Oh yes, I'm not letting you out of my sight," Lucy said. "You're where the action is."

It was dark by the time we reached the Love is a Splendored Thing Inn. We passed the sign, saying it was "for lovers who crave luxury."

"Nice place," Lucy commented. "Spencer has good taste."

"We're going to have to fly under the radar here. Act nonchalant."

"Gladie, you're blue."

She had a point. I stuck out like a sore thumb. "You have a point. Change of plans. Follow my lead."

We walked into the lobby. At first, the man at the counter didn't notice the blue woman enter with the southern belle in flowing peach organza. But then he did.

"May I…?" he asked, drifting off, his eyes never leaving my blueness.

I slapped my hand on the counter and flashed him my library card for a split second. "I'm Gladie Bolton with the CPD. We're here to review the crime scene."

"What's CPD?"

"Cannes Police Department." It wasn't a total lie. I was with Spencer, who was the chief of the Cannes Police Department.

"I thought the room was released and ready to be rented out," he said. He couldn't have been more than twenty years old, and he still had acne on his face. I would have bet money he would have preferred to be snooping around a murder scene instead of standing behind a counter.

"I'm from CSI Las Vegas," Lucy said. "There's always more to find. I can find blood in a grilled cheese sandwich."

"You can?"

"I could curl the hair on your chest with my stories," she

continued. "You ever hear of Charles Manson?"

"Yes," he breathed, his attention rapt.

"Me, too," she said.

"We just want to look around the room. It shouldn't take very long," I said and batted my blue eyelashes.

"I guess it can't hurt." He pushed a few buttons on his computer and walked around the counter, holding a key card. "Business has been slow since the murder," he explained, as he walked us to the room.

"We just want to make sure justice is served," Lucy said.

"I thought the husband did it with a steak knife. I heard he's in jail," the clerk said.

Lucy looked at me, and I shrugged.

"Just tying up loose ends," I said. "What have you heard about the husband?"

"I heard they were on their honeymoon. We get a lot of honeymooners or proposers. You know, when men propose marriage."

I suspected that was why Spencer had brought me there, too.

"Any idea why he killed her?" I asked.

"Maybe he had second thoughts about marriage?" he answered like a question.

That was reasonable. I was having second thoughts and third thoughts and fourth thoughts. Marriage was complicated.

"I can show you their room first. She wasn't killed there, though."

"Take us to the ice room first," I said.

"You want ice?"

Lucy and I spent hours searching the rooms for any clues about the murder, but the hotel had already cleaned it up, and nothing looked out of the ordinary. After a while, the hotel clerk left us alone to go back to the lobby.

"I'm a curse," Lucy said. "Whenever I'm around, all action stops."

"You're not a curse. This is my fault."

"At least you got to use the Bolton name. That was very exciting. How did it feel to say it?"

"It felt good," I said and giggled. We held hands and jumped up and down. Being happy was so much nicer with friends. But we had one friend who was in a terrible predicament, and I had to help her. I grew serious, again.

I closed my eyes and tried to make sense out of the murder. I retraced Mamie Foster's steps from her room to the ice machine and to my room. What could have happened to precipitate her murder?

"My Miss Marple is gone," I told Lucy, finally.

"Don't say that." She gave me a little shake. "Come on, Gladie. You can do it. Who stabbed this poor girl forty times and what does it have to do with Bridget?"

"I don't know," I said, giving up. I had never felt lower in my life. I was useless.

We returned to the lobby. "All done?" the clerk asked.

"I think so," I said.

"I forgot to tell you, there's one thing the police forgot to take with them," he said. "I guess they're not interested in it." He handed me a small, wooden paddle board with a ball attached to it with an elastic band. "I heard she was real good at it."

"How good?" I asked.

"Like she could paddle the hell out of the ball for days without stopping."

I grabbed Lucy's hand and gave it a squeeze. "Lucy, my Miss Marple just returned."

CHAPTER 16

When I was a little girl, my mother fell into a deep depression. That happened to her now and then because her third eye came with a big dose of empathy that was just too much for her. She felt others' pain, you see, dolly. Anyway, it got into her head that if the weather changed hard, it would wash her depression off her and blow it far away. So, she waited for a storm with her last glimmer of hope, and two weeks later, the storm came. I think it was the biggest storm in Cannes' history. It blew roofs off of houses, and it flooded the lake. The orchards were nothing but mud. Some people thought it was the end of the world, but my mother thought it was the beginning of hers. She wrapped a shmata around her shoulders and danced outside, welcoming the rain and wind to make her happy, again. And wouldn't you know it, bubbeleh? It did. She was happy for years afterward. It was a big lesson for me as a child. It taught me that sometimes we need a powerful storm to shake us back to where we need to be. A little destruction can heal the heart and soul. Tear it down to build it up. Sometimes that's the only way to a happy ending. That's some wisdom from me to you. Pass it on.

Lesson 133, Matchmaking advice from your Grandma Zelda

By the time Lucy and I got back to Cannes, the sun was coming up. I had called Spencer to let him know that I was with Lucy, and he told me that an alien broke into a house and was chased off by a dog.

"I think our alien problem is a home invader from planet Earth, Gladie. I want you home where it's safe," he told me on the phone.

"If he's breaking into houses, home isn't safe."

"Okay, then. I want you with me until we catch the bastard. I'll keep you safe. I have big muscles, you know. You want to see my muscles?"

"I've been intimate with your muscles," I said. It reminded me of Alice and her bragging about how strong she was.

"I'm serious," he said. "Come home."

"I'm on my way," I told him.

I got off the phone and told Lucy about the home invader.

"Home invasion in Cannes? We're becoming a big city, Gladie."

I didn't think we were becoming a big city. I thought evil liked small towns, too. But I wasn't surprised about the home invader not being an alien because it fit with my working theory about the murders.

The Mercedes swerved, and Lucy got the car under control. "Wow, the winds are strong," she said. "They're moving the car. And look at those clouds."

The sky was full of dark clouds and they were moving fast. "I think Grandma was right about the storm."

"It's supposed to be a beautiful Easter Sunday without a cloud in the sky. How's your Miss Marple doing? Do you know whodunit, yet?"

"I'm getting close."

"I can't wait. I want to be there when you tell the killer, 'You did it!' Maybe he'll make a run for it, and I can shoot him with my pearl-handled pistol."

"We can only hope," I said.

Lucy had to park her car away from Main Street because it was closed off for the Easter egg hunt. The wind had whipped up, and volunteers were fishing some of the decorations out of the trees. Lucy had to walk holding onto her dress because the wind was so bad, and it kept blowing it up over her head. "I feel like Marilyn Monroe," she said, happily. "Look, Gladie, the hunt has already started." She was right. Even though it was just after sunrise, the Easter egg hunt had already begun, but it wasn't like any Easter egg hunt I have ever heard about.

"Where are the kids?" I asked.

There were no kids. The town square was full of people, but none of them was less than seventy. There were old people in wheelchairs, old people pushing walkers, and a few walking with a cane. Each of them was holding an Easter basket, and they were collecting eggs at a painfully slow pace.

"Tell me I'm not going blind," Lucy said. "Tell me that I don't have cat scratch fever like Terri."

"I think I'm seeing it, too," I said.

"They've got my baskets. Gladie, what the devil's going on?"

We walked across the street to the small park. The mayor was watching the old people collect eggs. Next to him, the world record guy was taking notes.

"What the devil's going on?" Lucy repeated to the mayor.

"Hello! Hello! Mighty fine day. The Easter egg hunt is a big success. We're on our way to a world record. Isn't that so, Mr. Jones?"

"At this rate, I think you'll make it just under the wire," Mr. Jones said while he continued to scribble notes. "Good idea starting it at sunrise. You'll need the extra time, considering the physical limitations of your Easter egg hunters."

"Where are the children?" I asked.

"Little hiccough," the mayor said. "They decided not to come on account of Buckstars' front door."

We turned and looked at the door. The dildos were still stuck to it. "Superglue is amazing," Lucy said.

"The police won't let us remove them until the case is closed," the mayor said. "Obviously, the chief doesn't care about Easter," he said, looking at me.

I shrugged. "I don't know about police procedure."

"Not important. Not important," he said. "We don't need children for our Easter egg hunt. I found replacements. The Cannes Retirement Community was only too happy to help us out."

"This is the saddest thing I've ever seen," Lucy said. "I love this crazy town."

"We're going to break this world record, you mark my words," he said. "Come by in a couple hours. We're having live accordion music."

"And there's a celebrity from England, too," I said.

"Yes, well..." the mayor said and turned away.

The wind whipped up, and one of the old folks' wheelchairs went flying down the street. "We got another runner!" one of the volunteers yelled, and about five people ran after the chair.

"I think I'm ready for coffee," I told Lucy. We hadn't slept all night, and the cold wind was chapping my lips.

We crossed the street back to Tea Time. Inside, it was doing bang up business. There must have been sixty people crammed into the small shop and no place left to sit. Every person had one of Lucy's baskets filled with eggs. We squeezed our way to the bar. Ruth had worked up a sweat from waiting on everyone and Julie was serving the tables, dropping half of the cups and squeaking "Uh oh!" each time one crashed to the floor.

"I'm going to be bankrupt at this rate," Ruth complained to me. "Whose idea was this stupid thing, anyway? They're all resting their titanium hips in here, pretending they're searching for eggs."

"And Grandma says a storm is coming," I said.

"Well, that's just perfect, then. So, they'll be hiding from that, too. Old people like me can't be out in the weather all day, you know. If that mayor of ours was any dumber, his brain would be made of vanilla pudding. Hell, it probably is made of vanilla pudding. The sugar free kind with the aftertaste."

"Ruth, where's my tea?" an old man demanded next to me. "I've been waiting forever."

Ruth scowled at him. "You've been waiting forever? That's a long time, Christopher. How long is forever exactly to you? More than two minutes?"

"I've never met a woman more unpleasant than you, Ruth Fletcher," he growled.

"Trust me, I can get a whole lot more unpleasant if you don't wait patiently for your tea, Christopher."

The man blanched. "All right. All right. I'll wait over there, patiently."

"Here, take these cookies with you," she said, handing him a plate. "No need for you to starve."

Ruth might have been unpleasant, but she had a good heart. The door opened, and the mayor walked in, along with a big wind that blew through the shop. "Let's keep the hunt going. We're falling behind schedule," the mayor sang.

There was a chorus of grumbling, but the group began to get up and walk outside. "We should probably help them," I told Lucy.

"Don't bother," Ruth said. "This thing is going to last another forty-five minutes. An hour tops."

"I don't mind hunting for some eggs," Lucy said. "But let's get caffeine in us first."

With most of Tea Time cleared out, Ruth served us quickly and then sat with us at a corner table. The celebrity from England was sitting at the next table and telling a story to some locals.

"My record has held for the past ten years," he said. "And they measure me each year to make sure I haven't grown at all."

"Doesn't that beat all," a man at the table said.

"Someone measures you?" a woman asked. "With a measuring tape?"

Ruth leaned closer to Lucy and me. "That man over there is a Paramount World Records holder, but you'll never guess for what."

"Longest tongue," Lucy said.

"Longest toenail," I said.

"Are you two playing with me?" Ruth sneered. "It's not the longest. It's the shortest. Guess what's the shortest."

"Shortest," Lucy repeated. "Shortest, shortest, shortest. Nooooo…" she said, staring at the celebrity from England.

"Yes," Ruth said. "The emcee celebrity for our Easter egg hunt's claim to fame is that he has the world's shortest how do you do. That'll put this town on the map for sure. The mayor had no idea, of course, until yesterday when it was too late to find someone else. Once he found out, he almost swallowed his tongue."

"There seems to be a penis theme to our town, lately," Lucy said. "Have you noticed? Gladie? Gladie, are you listening?"

"Yes," I said. "Sorry, I was drifting."

"Gladie has figured out who the killer is," Lucy told Ruth. "She's got a brilliant investigative mind."

"Well? Spit it out, girl. Who's the killer?" Ruth asked.

"Not Bridget," I said.

"Well, of course not Bridget. Only an idiot would think that girl would stab a man. So, who did it?"

There was a loud crack of thunder, and the wind whistled loudly. "I have to give it to Zelda," Ruth said. "That's going to be some storm."

There was more thunder, and then we could hear screaming. "What on earth is that?" Ruth asked.

We walked outside to see what was going on. The rain was coming down in sheets, and the wind was howling. "I've had enough!" a man shouted. "Screw Easter!" He threw his basket onto the ground and marched away with his cane. He wasn't the only one. There was a rebellion going on with Easter baskets being thrown to the ground all over.

The mayor headed off one of the men and tried to stop him, grabbing onto his arm. "We're almost there. Don't stop now. Come on, townsfolk! We can do this!"

"Get your hands off of me," the man said, but the mayor wouldn't let go. The rest of the egg hunters stopped what they were doing. The tension was palpable. It looked like the enthusiasm for volunteering had flown the coop, and it was replaced by good, old-fashioned irritation. I looked around as more than one person held up an egg like it was a baseball, and they were ready to bean the mayor in the head.

"We probably should go inside," Ruth said just as the eggs started to fly. One after the other, the eggs became projectiles, as the egg hunters threw them with all of their strength. It was a free for all. Every tired senior citizen on Main Street was launching painted, hard-boiled eggs.

"My eggs!" Josephine yelled. "I spent a week preparing those eggs! Oh, my poor eggs."

She broke down in sobs, and I had to admit to myself that I was slightly happy to see it, considering that she had painted me blue.

The egg fight degenerated quickly, and I was hit in the stomach with one. "Take cover!" Lucy yelled. "Hey, this dress is from Neiman Marcus!"

There were police sirens and Main Street was invaded by most of the police force. Spencer spotted me and marched in my direction. "Get inside, Pinky. Get inside, now."

Everyone without an egg went into Tea Time for shelter. "Didn't I tell you to go home?" Spencer demanded from me.

"I wanted a latte first."

The mayor, the world records guy, and the entire Easter egg hunt committee came into Tea Time, and they all had a look of total defeat on their faces.

"It was a good try," the world record guy told the mayor. "You almost made it."

"But the day isn't over," the mayor pleaded.

"Give it a rest," Josephine said. "It's the Battle of the Bulge out there." She plopped down on a chair. "I'm done with committees. Done with volunteering. From now on, I'm doing the quilting bee and the book club, and that's it."

The lights flickered, and the wind howled.

I sat down at a table, too. Alice sat down next to me. "So, have you seen any more dead people?" she asked me.

"Just the three this week," I said.

"She knows who the killer is," Lucy said. "She's Miss Marple, you know."

"Oh, she does, does she?" Spencer asked.

"Nosy Parker," Josephine grumbled.

"She knows you so well," Spencer told me.

"I think I know who the killer is," I said. Everyone in the shop turned to me. Spencer smirked his little smirk, stretched his legs out, and laced his fingers behind his head.

"I've got time while my men clear up the mess outside," he

said.

"Oh, yes, tell us who the killer is," Alice said.

"We were so close to breaking the record," the mayor moaned.

"I've held a world record for ten years," the celebrity from England said.

Lucy shushed them both. "Go on, Gladie. Show them what you've got."

The group adjusted their chairs, as if I was the headliner at a Vegas show. I didn't like to be the center of attention, but I had been rolling around my suspicions in my head since the night before, and I was dying to let them out.

"I may be wrong," I started. "I've been wrong a lot this past week. "It started with the dead woman in my bed."

There was a gasp in the room.

"They said her husband had killed her, but I didn't believe that. And I was right. But I couldn't focus on that because my best friend was accused of killing Bradford Blythe. I knew she didn't kill him, but I couldn't figure out who did. The obvious suspect in my mind was Ford Essex. He had looked at Brad sideways, and Ford told me that he was in business with him. Funny business, I thought. Then there was my contractor. He was in business with Brad, too."

"He was?" Spencer asked.

"Then, we found out that Ford was smuggling drugs, and I figured that the three of them, along with Liz, were doing it together and Brad's murder was just business. But Josephine had mentioned seeing a dead body, and I wondered if she was talking about Ethel's dead body, which she said was under Buckstars. And then there was Alice, who liked to talk about how she would kill someone."

"I like the stabbing idea," Alice said.

"And the voice," I continued.

"What voice?" Josephine asked.

"There was a voice in Buckstars, talking about killing someone. Later I realized it was Griffin. So, I figured he was the killer, but who killed him? Ford and Liz were in jail, so it wasn't them. Again, I knew it wasn't Bridget. Did I leave anything out? Oh, yeah, the aliens. Why were people complaining about being attacked? None of it tied together. None of it made sense. Everything seemed upside down and backward."

"It was random," Spencer breathed, catching on.

"It was random," I agreed. "At least sort of."

"So, that's when I went back to the first murder, and it became clear when I saw this." I pulled the paddle out of my purse and held it up. "See? You get it?"

"What is it?" Alice asked.

"Is this a joke?" Josephine asked.

"It's a paddle. She was good at..." I started.

The lights flickered and went out. Someone grabbed me from behind and began to drag me. I fought against him and screamed, but he was stronger than me. A shot rang out, and I felt a sting in my arm.

"Gladie!" Spencer yelled.

The lights came back on. I had been dragged behind the tea cozy rack, and the killer was holding a knife to my throat. "I knew it was you," I said.

"Be quiet," he said.

"Good luck with that," I heard, and I looked up to see Spencer pointing a gun at my attacker. "Put down the knife, or I'll blow a hole through your head."

"Mamie Foster could paddle a ball for days," I explained with the knife still to my throat. "Get it? Paddling a ball for days was a world record, and then it all fit. Gregory Jones, representative of Paramount World Records travels to verify records. He was at the Inn to see Mamie paddle, and he killed her there."

"Why?" Lucy asked from across the tea shop.

"Because he likes killing. Don't you see? He's a serial killer. He killed Brad. He killed Griffin. And half the time he was terrible at it, and he would miss when he tried to break into houses and sometimes he got so frustrated that he would kill an animal. It was him, not aliens. That's why it didn't make any sense in my mind. Because he's crazy and doesn't make any sense. Except for the first murder. That murder tied him in perfectly. I guess I needed a little logic before I could solve the mystery."

I took a deep breath. I felt euphoric. My Miss Marple mojo was back in full force. I was so ecstatic that I more or less had forgotten that a serial killer was going to kill me.

"You're going to let me out of here, or I'm going to slit her throat," he threatened.

"I'm not going to let that happen," Spencer said.

"What do you mean?" I asked. "You're not going to let him out of here or you're not going to let him slit my throat?"

"I'm serious," he threatened, again. "I'll kill her!"

"Now would be a good time to shoot him," I told Spencer.

He didn't have time to shoot him. Just then, the door opened, and Terri Williams, victim of cat scratch fever, ran in. "You did this to me, Gladie Burger!" she shouted like a wild banshee. "I'm going to get you for this!"

Sometimes, it's not easy being me.

Terri came at me like a bull charging a matador but with much bigger hair. The serial killer World Records guy flinched in fear and pulled back. I did, too, just as Terri reached us, stepping out of her line of attack. That's how she overshot and landed on the serial killer instead of me and took him down to the floor, going at him like a wildcat. The knife flew out of his hand and landed on the floor on the other side of the bar.

Spencer pulled me behind him. "Why don't we do dinner and a movie like other couples?" he asked me.

The door opened again, and this time it was my match, Bruce Coyle. "I love you, Terri!" he shouted and made a beeline for her. "I'll save you!"

We watched as he punched the serial killer in the jaw, knocking him out and pulled Terri into his arms. "Terri, my Terri," he said, hugging her to him. Her eyes rolled around, as if she was trying to focus. Her face had long scratches on it, but she was still beautiful.

"Bruce?" she asked, slowly coming back to her senses. "Is that you?" The crazy had left her eyes, and I wondered if it was the power of love that had finally cured her cat scratch fever. A tear rolled down my cheek with the realization that I had succeeded in making a love match.

"Oh, Terri," Bruce cooed at her. "You've come back to me. I'm so sorry about my cat."

"What about your cat?"

"Will you marry me?"

Terri seemed to notice me for the first time since she had regained her sanity. "Gladie, why are you blue?"

"If anybody can explain to me what the hell is going on, I'll pay you ten dollars," Ruth announced to the tea shop.

"I think Terri is a serial killer," Alice answered.

Lucy skipped toward me with her pearl-handled gun clutched in her hand. She gave me a hug. "Finally, I got to see the action," she said, joyfully. "It was even better than I had imagined."

"Did you shoot me?" I asked, looking at her gun.

"Did I? I was aiming for the world record guy."

"Gladie, your arm is bleeding," Spencer told me, pointing at my arm. I looked down.

"Holy shit, I've been shot."

And I passed out.

I was in bed, watching *Murder, She Wrote* and eating Cheetos from a family-sized bag when my grandmother walked in. "Well, it's been ten days, and I'm right as rain," she told me. "Back to work with me. How are you feeling?"

I pointed at the bandage on my arm. "Better. Can you

hold down the fort while I'm recovering?"

"I think I can manage."

Meryl's parrot flew into the room, landed on the television, and said something I couldn't understand.

"Estonian," my grandmother said. "We finally figured it out."

"I think I heard Liz Essex speaking it. Do you think they had him for two years?"

"I think so. I heard the parrot say 'orgia' which means orgy in Estonian."

"So, they were swingers, drug smugglers, and birdnappers."

"But not killers," Grandma said, always looking on the bright side.

Spencer walked into the room and plopped onto the bed. "What are we watching?" he asked, changing the channel to a baseball game. "And why is there a parrot on my new TV?"

"I hear that you're looking for a new detective," my grandmother said to Spencer.

He took a handful of Cheetos from my bag. "Yep. Terri's left town to work in pesticides with her new husband, so I'm out a cop. Why? Do you have anyone in mind?"

"I might. I'll get back to you about it."

She left the room, and Spencer gave me a Cheetos-flavored kiss. "When Terri quit, I found the tickets."

"What tickets?" I asked. "I know nothing about no stinkin' tickets."

"Nobody lies better than you, Pinky. Anyway, I got rid of them so you don't have to sell a kidney to pay for them."

"You're so romantic."

He took my ring hand and brought it to his lips. "I guess we have to start talking about China patterns."

"We do? Is that a rule?"

"You're not backing out on this marriage thing are you?" he asked. He was playing it off like he was joking, but I sensed that he was worried.

"Never. You and me are forever, Spencer. But I might back out of China patterns."

"Most women would die for a China pattern."

"What you don't know about women could fill an encyclopedia."

He pulled me in close to him. "Let me show you about how I can fill an encyclopedia."

"You are five years old," I said, but I got goosebumps thinking about it.

There was a sound in the doorway, and I sat up to see Bridget holding a thick stack of papers. "I'm not interrupting anything, am I?" she asked.

"Bridget, are you all right? Is the baby okay?" I asked.

"Yes, I came to show you my manifesto. I think we should make copies and send them to news outlets."

She sat down on the chair next to the bed. "What news outlets?" I asked.

"All of them," she said. "You want me to read you what I wrote? I think it's groundbreaking and earth shattering."

"Oh, God," Spencer groaned.

"There's a section about God in it, too," she said.

I eyed the thick stack on her lap. "How many pages did you write, Bridget?"

"Only five-hundred-sixty. It's the first volume. I figure there will be four volumes. Ready? Here we go. 'Chapter one: Patriarchy in the Arrests of Innocent Women.'"

"I think she's talking about you," I told Spencer.

"Seriously, consider dinner and a movie for once," he said and held me as we listened to Bridget's manifesto.

And don't forget to sign up for the newsletter for new releases and special deals: http://www.elisesax.com/mailing-list.php

The story continues with book nine, *The Big Kill.*

ABOUT THE AUTHOR

Elise Sax worked as a journalist for fifteen years, mostly in Paris, France. She took a detour from journalism and became a private investigator before writing her first novel. She lives in Southern California with her two sons.

She loves to hear from her readers. Don't hesitate to contact her at elisesax@gmail.com, and sign up for her newsletter at http://elisesax.com/mailing-list.php to get notifications of new releases and sales.

Elisesax.com
https://www.facebook.com/ei.sax.9
@theelisesax